DEMON'S DELIGHT

A Bewitching Bedlam Novella

YASMINE GALENORN

A Nightqueen Enterprises LLC Publication

Published by Yasmine Galenorn

PO Box 2037, Kirkland WA 98083-2037

DEMON'S DELIGHT

A Bewitching Bedlam Novella

Copyright © 2020 by Yasmine Galenorn

First Electronic Printing: 2020 Nightqueen Enterprises LLC

First Print Edition: 2020 Nightqueen Enterprises, LLC

Cover Art & Design: Ravven

Editor: Elizabeth Flynn

ALL RIGHTS RESERVED No part of this book may be reproduced or distributed in any format, be it print or electronic or audio, without permission. Please prevent piracy by purchasing only authorized versions of this book.

This is a work of fiction. Any resemblance to actual persons, living or dead, businesses, or places is entirely coincidental and not to be construed as representative or an endorsement of any living/ existing group, person, place, or business.

A Nightqueen Enterprises LLC Publication

Published in the United States of America

ACKNOWLEDGMENTS

Thanks to my beloved husband, Samwise, who is more supportive than any husband out there. (Hey, I'm biased!) He believes in me, even at times when I'm having trouble believing in myself. Thank you to my wonderful assistants—Andria Holley and Jennifer Arnold. And to my friends—namely Carol, Jade, Jo, Shawntelle, and Mandy. Also, to the whole UF Group and Romance Groups that I'm in. They've been an infinite system of support

Love and scritches to my four furbles—Caly, Brighid (the cat, not the goddess), Morgana, and li'l boy Apple, who make every day a delight. And reverence, honor, and love to my spiritual guardians—Mielikki, Tapio, Ukko, Rauni, and Brighid (the goddess, not the cat).

And to you, readers, for taking Maddy and Aegis and Bubba into your heart. Be cautious when you rub a kitty's belly—you never know when you might end up petting a cjinn! I hope you enjoy this book. If you want to know more about me and my work, check out my bibliography in the back of the book, be sure to sign up for my newsletter, and you can find me on the web at Galenorn.com. And if you love this book, I'd really appreciate it you can leave a review for me!

WELCOME TO DEMON'S DELIGHT

It's approaching the most wonderful time of the year again—Yule—and Bedlam is up to its ears in snow and manic joy. Maddy and Sandy are planning a double wedding, but things go haywire when someone unexpected shows up, one who's intent on winning Maddy away from Aegis. If that wasn't enough to deal with, something is turning the town of Bedlam on its head with a bout of rogue magic. Now, between the chaos running rampant and a choice Maddy never expected to face, will she make it to the altar before disaster strikes?

CHAPTER ONE

The holiday rush hit us hard, but we were weathering it with ease. Every room in the Bewitching Bedlam was spoken for, and we were booked through the New Year. I had started a waiting list, in case we had any cancellations.

Word had gotten out that Aegis was part owner and his groupies were booking rooms just to be near their fantasy crush. It was good for business, but problematic as far as some of the more eager female guests went. We'd had to turn out a couple of them for walking around the house in their underwear, and one woman even tried to sneak down into the basement to look for his lair.

Because my rib was still healing and my hip was still bruised, thanks to my freakshow ex-husband, I couldn't do much except supervise. So Kelson hired two interns from the Neverfall Academy for Gifted Students. She kept them busy, leaving me free for admin duties, as well as to plan for my wedding.

Today marked my first time out of the house in a

while. My best friend Sandy and I were downtown, shopping for wedding accessories. We had quickly realized that a double wedding had to accommodate four people's tastes, not just two.

I was wearing a corset to help stabilize my ribs, and was using a cane because my hip was still cranky, but at least I was out in public.

"I swear, I've been going stir-crazy," I said, as Sandy helped me out of the car. We'd managed to find a spot right in front of the French Pair—a lingerie shop.

"Cabin fever?" She grinned. "I'll bet you've been a delight to be around lately." Sandy had been my BFF since 1699, when we first met. We had come to America together, after one hell of a spate of fighting vampires and running wild with satyrs.

"Yeah, and after being shut up in the house for several weeks, the town seems like a palatial expanse."

I paused by the side of the car. I needed to talk to Sandy about something, but it could wait until lunch. As I leaned against the door, a gust of fresh air washed over me. The weather was cold and snowy, and the town looked like a winter wonderland. That sounded cliché, but it was true.

Located at the northernmost point of the San Juan Islands, Bedlam Island had been founded by witches a long time ago, and the combination of the location along with all the magical energy in the town drew in storms like a magnet. Whether it was wind, rain, or snow, Bedlam was a hotbed of meteorological activity.

Bedlam was both the name of the island and the town, and the Pretcom congregated here. A few humans lived on the island, but mostly witches and satyrs, and shifters and Fae folk called Bedlam home. We had a few vampires, too, although they weren't quite as welcome, except for Aegis. Not only was he my fiancé, he was a musician and popular in the clubbing culture.

"You all right?" Sandy asked as I winced.

"Yeah, the stitch in my side catches me off guard, but Jordan says I need to start moving around. He didn't suggest running any marathons, but the more I move, the better off I'll be." I straightened and, using the cane more for balance than support, followed Sandy into the store.

THE FRENCH PAIR WAS AN UPSCALE BOUTIQUE, specializing in lingerie for special occasions. And you couldn't get much more special than a wedding.

Bree Silverlight—one of the Summer Fae—had recently taken over the shop. Her eyes lit up as she saw us. "Maddy, Sandy! What can I do for you today? Rumor has it you're both getting hitched. Any chance you're shopping for your wedding trousseaus?"

"There's every chance, Bree," I said, returning her smile. While Fae glamour didn't work on witches, Bree's joy was still infectious.

"What color scheme? Somehow, I don't picture either of you as the white-lace type."

"Right again," Sandy said. She was a blonde, with hair down to her shoulders and the body of a fitness guru. She was trim, tall, tanned, and wore yoga pants and a crop top everywhere. She was also a business mogul and smart as a whip. "Pastels—blue and green are my favorites."

I, on the other hand, was shorter than Sandy, pale, and

definitely well-padded. My hair was the color of a black cat on Halloween. "I do better with gem tones. Purple, green, burgundy…"

Bree went into overdrive, piling teddies and bustiers and gowns into her arms. "I'll bring these to the dressing room. What size do you need?"

While we waited, I sat down on the bench. My side ached. I was probably overdoing it, but it felt so good to be out that I didn't want to go home. A little pain was worth the freedom.

"I've got a problem," Sandy said.

"What's up?" Given all we had been through, it could be anything. "Jenna's all right, isn't she? And Max?"

"Yes, Jenna's fine, and so is Max. It's just…well…Max's parents are coming to visit. We've never met and I'm terrified they won't like me."

"That's ridiculous. Everybody loves you."

"Not them, I'm afraid. Max warned me that they're conservative, but I didn't realize how old-school they are. They aren't happy that he's marrying me. They liked Gracie enough, but they weren't happy that she was a witch and not a tiger-shifter. But when she died, they expected him to remarry someone from their pride. Now, he's chosen *another* witch instead of a shifter, and they've been…*vocal* in their objections."

"He told you all this?" I was surprised. Max did everything he could to make Sandy happy and that he would actually tell her about their objections surprised me.

She shook her head. "No, I overheard them. He was in the next room, FaceTiming with them. I was passing by when I heard his mother complaining that now she'll never get the grandchildren she's been waiting for. He told them he was going to adopt Jenna after we got married, so they'd have a grandchild."

"What did they say?" I dreaded the answer. Shifters could be pretty rigid in their resistance to interspecies marriages.

"His father said that she wouldn't be bloodkin and that Max should find a woman who could keep the family line going." Her eyes watered as she tried to blink back the tears.

The look on her face broke my heart. I wanted to track down Max's parents and beat them senseless. "I'd like to hex his ass. So what did Max say?"

"He stood up for me. And yes, by this time I was hiding behind the door, listening to everything they said. They argued and in the end his parents cut the conversation short. When Max came out of the office, he was in one hell of a mood. He didn't tell me what happened and I couldn't very well ask since I'd been eavesdropping." She shrugged. "I hate that his *family* thinks I'm not good enough for him."

I nodded. Families could be problematic, especially when it came to weddings. "Are they coming to the ceremony?"

"I think so. I wish they weren't."

"Do they know it's a double wedding? If they don't like the fact that you're a witch, they'll just love that their son is getting married alongside another witch and a vampire."

There had never been any question that Sandy and I would have a double wedding. The guys had agreed from the start. On New Year's Eve, at twilight, we were getting married in the backyard of the Bewitching Bedlam. We had opted for a theme of red, black, and white. The men would be dressed in black, we'd be dressed in red, and the snow would provide the white backdrop to everything.

And there was plenty of snow. Bedlam had been slammed by a storm in early December that had left the entire island stranded. Two feet of snow covered the island and everything sparkled like a field of frozen diamonds. Since then, we'd had two more storms.

"I don't know. What makes me angriest is that they won't accept Jenna. It's one thing to call *me* a bitch and tell me you don't think I'm worthy, but it's a whole different matter when you attack my daughter." Sandy had pushed through the adoption papers quickly, and Jenna was now legally her daughter. Both had been thrilled. "They practically called us Dirt Witches."

Dirt Witches? That was an insult above and beyond good taste. "Real classy. I'm surprised you didn't grab the phone from Max and cuss them out."

"I thought about it."

"If they cause any trouble, that's the last event on this island they'll ever attend. I like Max, but *nobody* messes up my wedding—or hurts my best friend in the process."

As she stared at the floor, I leaned forward. "You have to talk to Max about this before his parents arrive."

Sandy gave me a shrug, standing as Bree approached the dressing room door.

"I know," she said. "I realize that. But it's not going to be easy. Max was brought up to respect the Pride."

"Of course he was, but he made it work with Gracie and he can smooth it over for you. Interactions with relatives never are easy. I admit I'm grateful Aegis doesn't have any living relatives that we know of."

Sandy took a deep breath and nodded. "We'll get through it."

At that moment, Bree opened the door and peeked her head in. "Here you go."

A half hour and countless items later, Sandy and I left the shop with several bags each. I'd picked up three nightgowns, two bras, and a couple corset tops with matching panties. Sandy had found two nighties, a teddy, and a pair of silk pajamas.

"Where to next?" she asked as we piled our loot in the trunk of the Lexus I was renting. My CRV was too high for me to get into with my injured hip and rib, and Aegis's Corvette was too low and cramped.

"We have to decide on flowers, so let's…" I paused as a noise from up the street caught my attention. "What's going on up there?"

Sandy frowned, shading her eyes. "I don't know."

"Let's go find out." I wasn't just being nosy. The Moonrise Coven was in charge of Bedlam, and since I was High Priestess, that meant I was on the city council. What went on in this town was my business.

We started toward the corner, cautious on the icy sidewalks. Even though the shop owners cleared them, black ice built up incredibly fast. A half block away, two sidewalk Santas were going at it. They were in the middle of the snowbank alongside the curb, trying to beat each other senseless.

"What the ever-loving fuck?" I asked.

One of the men had blood spilling out from a busted lip. His fake white beard was a blotchy mess. The other was wheezing so hard I wondered if he was going to have a heart attack. A number of shoppers had gathered around, shouting, egging on the fight. A few children were crying.

"Crap on a shingle," Sandy muttered. "I wonder if anybody's called Delia yet?"

Delia Walters, a straw-blond werewolf, was the sheriff *and* the mayor, and she did a good job of taking care of the island's security.

"I will." I pulled out my phone.

But before I could get my phone to my ear, the sound of sirens echoed as a patrol car came shrieking down the street. Delia swerved to the side, parking right beside the snow dune, and she and a tall deputy—Derek Lindsey—jumped out. They waded into the fray, shouting as they separated the Santas.

"Break it up!" Delia was short, but she was strong and people in the town respected her. "What the hell are you two doing? I told you yesterday, *no brawling in the streets*!"

Both men stared up at her, looking dazed. One of them hiccupped and the smell of stale whiskey wafted off of him.

"You're drunk?" I said. "You're supposed to be *Santa Claus*, not some rummy on the street!"

Delia shook her head. "I knew it had to be this pair when I got the call."

"What are they fighting over?" I asked.

"Turf war. The drunk Santa is from Yuletide Cheer, a donation center for toys for the kids. The other one's from Crystal Chimes. They were at it two days ago. Apparently, this street corner has the best draw for donors, and only one person at a time is allowed to solicit on this spot." Delia stared at the men. "I warned you that the next time you were both ending up in the slammer."

She motioned to Derek. "Cuff them, read them their rights, and put them in the car. Take their donation buckets and have somebody deliver them to their respective charities."

Derek maneuvered both men into the back of the patrol car. He put the buckets in the trunk.

"How are you doing?" Delia asked me. "I know you're still feeling rough around the edges."

I shrugged, wincing as my rib pulled a little. "Like a trussed turkey. My rib's still cracked. Hip is healing up, but Craig bruised me up pretty badly. He could kick like a son of a bitch. Today's my first day out of the house and it's wonderful, despite the twinges. We're shopping for wedding accessories."

Sandy gave me a long look. "You've been on your feet a lot today. We should sit down somewhere. Let's eat lunch before we drop in at the florist."

As we said good-bye to Delia and headed for the car, the weather shifted and the snow began to fall again, big, fat flakes drifting down to add yet another layer on what we already had. I caught one on my tongue. I was a kid at heart, even though I was on the upper side of three hundred. Sandy laughed and did the same. I gently stretched out my arms, looking up into the falling fluff.

"I love snow. I love winter," I said. "All right, where should we eat?"

"How about the new place that opened up a couple weeks ago? The Mussel Bar? Why don't you let me drive?" She waited to make sure I was in the car before sliding into the driver's seat.

"Lead the way," I said. A steaming bowl of clam chowder sounded perfect.

As we settled into the booth and placed our orders —clam chowder, cheese bread, and an appetizer of calamari—I leaned my head back against the seat.

"I've got a problem myself, but I wanted to wait until we were out of the house. Aegis is asleep, but I didn't want Kelson to overhear." I opened my purse and withdrew an envelope.

"What's wrong?"

"I received this a couple days ago. I don't know what to think." I pushed the envelope across the table.

Sandy stared at it for a moment, then picked it up and glanced at the front. "It was sent from Bedlam, so it's from someone in town." She opened it and shook out the single piece of paper that was inside. As she opened it up, she gasped. "What the hell is this?"

"That's what *I* want to know."

She laid the page down on the table so we could both look at it.

Maddy, I love you. I love you so much and it kills me that we're not together. You know you don't belong with him. You were meant to be mine, and I won't stop until we're together. Let him go or I'll make him leave. I'm the one you were meant to be with. I'm the one who can make your dreams come true.

"Do you know who sent this?" She looked up at me. "There's no name, and no return address."

I shook my head. "I have no idea, but Sandy, I don't think this is a prank. Whoever wrote the note is unbalanced and dangerous. I can feel it."

As the waitress brought our food I slid the letter back into the envelope. We waited until she had set out our chowder and bread and calamari and drinks.

After she left, Sandy took a sip of her tea. "Does anybody have a crush on you? What about Ralph? He's usually behind these stupid stunts."

"No," I said. "It's not Ralph. For one thing, he's head over heels about Ivy Vine. And two… Ralph may be a big dumb goofus, but I don't think he'd pull this sort of stunt."

As we set to our lunches, it felt like a cloud had settled over our heads. Only this one didn't have snow. This cloud was dark and full of thunder and lightning. A storm was brewing, only I didn't know when or where it would hit.

CHAPTER TWO

By the time we had picked out flowers, I was ready to go home. We had settled on lily of the valley, ferns, and baby's breath for the décor. I would carry a bouquet of red roses, fern, and white chrysanthemums. Sandy's bouquet would be white roses, fern, and red chrysanthemums.

When we got back to my house, Sandy carried my packages in for me, then poured two glasses of wine while I eased myself down into the rocking chair. Kelson brought us a tray of gingerbread men, sugar cookies, and chocolate-mint petit fours.

Aegis had been baking up a storm, filling the house with the scents of cinnamon and apples, pumpkin and peppermint. Having a fiancé who was one of the best bakers in town was a plus. Every night, when he wasn't at rehearsal, he'd be baking goodies for our bed and breakfast.

As Sandy and I settled down with spirits and cookies, I

leaned back, thinking what an odd path my life had followed.

MY NAME IS MAUDLIN GALLOWGLASS—MADDY FOR SHORT. The line in that old folk song, "Mad Tom of Bedlam," was written about me: *Mad Maudlin goes on dirty toes, for to save her shoes from gravel.* Regardless of the speculation on who the author was, I know for a fact. My ex-boyfriend—once the love of my life—Tom wrote it about us and our journeys.

But Tom was caught by vampires in 1720 and they turned him. That's when my rampage through the UK and Europe began. I was one of the most terrifying vampire hunters to ever exist.

Mad Maudlin, indeed.

I hated the creatures so much that I banded together with Sandy and Fata Morgana and we tore through town and country, in a frenzy of destruction. We were known as the *Witches Wild,* and on we went, my desire for revenge fueling our passion.

Then, on the last night we went hunting, we found a nest of them. I rained down fire and brimstone on the village, killing almost all of them who were there. I was possessed by the fire, a trail of blood in my wake. At that moment, I truly *was* Mad Maudlin—by fury and revenge. But at the pinnacle of my rage, Fata and Sandy drew me back from the edge.

That night, my anger died out with the last embers of the village. I knew it was time to put away my stake, or I would slip into a dark abyss from which there would be no return.

I opted to put away the stake.

Fata Morgana fled out to sea. She still lives out on the waves. She's turning into a goddess, a force of the Ocean Mother. I don't envy her.

As for me? I've learned that not all vampires are evil. Over the past couple hundred years I've learned how to be happy. And I've found love.

Sandy and I are still best friends. I own a bed and breakfast on Bedlam Island. And I'm in love with Aegis, my beloved vampire. He's a singer and a baker, and he has his own tragic backstory. Together, we've helped heal each other. Something deeper than love drew us together. It's as though we have been around together before, in a different life. Our bond is core-deep. So, we're getting married. And while my life isn't perfect, I'm happy.

And life is what it is. Knock wood it stays that way.

"Flowers are checked off the list." Sandy sipped the cabernet.

"That's one more thing settled. How's your dress coming, by the way? We don't have much time." I glanced at the calendar. New Year's was coming up quickly.

"It's almost finished. I tried it on again yesterday and it's gorgeous."

"Mermaid style, right?"

Sandy grinned. "Right. I just can't pull off the ball gown look like you can."

My own dress, which was hanging in the closet in a

dustproof bag, was a crimson princess ball gown, satin beneath a lace-over-tulle skirt. It had a second overskirt—again, lace on tulle. The gown was strapless, with a fitted sweetheart-neck bodice that was embossed with tone-on-tone roses. Sandy's dress would be true red, given the warmer undertones to her skin.

"The guys have their tuxes. I'm just hoping I can manage through the Winter Solstice ritual." Because I was the High Priestess of the Moonrise Coven, I was expected to lead the town's ritual. We had scaled back on the extravagance, given my injuries, and Sandy would shoulder the majority of the work to take some of the strain off of me, but it was still going to draw a lot of energy.

The Moonrise Coven had been intricately linked to Bedlam since 1950, when it was founded. Back then, the High Priestess had been the city mayor as well.

We were responsible for running the rituals for the solstices and equinoxes. The other four Sabbats were left to private ritual. The coven was also responsible for keeping a leash on the vampires who lived on the island, and we had the authority to mete out punishment to them.

Essie Vanderbilt, the Queen of the Pacific Northwest Vampire Nation, had controlled the previous High Priestess like a puppet, but now that I was on the job, Essie and I had developed an uneasy truce.

As if reading my mind, Sandy said, "Have you head from Essie lately?"

I shrugged. "She RSVP'd for the wedding." I paused. Sandy was staring at her goblet, a pensive look on her face. "What's going on? There has to be more than just Max's parents."

Sandy shrugged. "Yeah, there is. Jenna's running around with a group of students I don't approve of. I'm afraid she's going to get in trouble."

Jenna was Sandy's adopted daughter. She was barely into her teens and her mother had dropped her on Sandy's doorstep before running off and getting herself killed on one of her many world-hopping adventures. Jenna was smart and talented, but heading into that invincible state kids always went through, where they thought they knew everything and that nothing could hurt them.

"That doesn't sound like Jenna," I said.

"Yeah, well, I didn't think so either, but there you go." She glanced at the clock. "I'd better get going. I'm meeting Max for dinner at Zweb's Steakhouse. If we go to my restaurant, all I'll end up doing is working through dinner."

As I saw her out, I noticed that it was beginning to snow again. The world was blanketed in white, and the snow had a magical feel to it. Breathing in a lungful of the chill air, I shut the door and went to help Kelson sort out what we were serving for dinner.

CHAPTER THREE

Kelson was looking through the refrigerator. We normally planned menus a week in advance, but somehow, life had gotten away from us this past week and we were running on a day-to-day basis. "What do you think of pot roast for dinner?" Kelson asked. "We haven't made that for a couple weeks. I think everybody would enjoy it."

Guests at the Bewitching Bedlam had their choice of eating out, or eating dinner in. They had to let us know by ten A.M. whether they'd be in for dinner. We provided breakfast as a matter of course. We currently had seven guests, and all the guestrooms were filled. For a change, everybody had opted to eat dinner in at the B&B, so we'd have a full table. Aegis had made three apple pies the night before, so we had plenty of dessert.

"Pot roast sounds like a wonderful idea. Do we have time to make it?"

"If I put it in the pressure cooker, we do. It will only take an hour that way. I'll roast the vegetables in the oven, and add them after the meat is done. When Aegis wakes up he can make a batch of dinner rolls, and if I throw together a salad, that should work." She paused, then added, "Oh, there's a letter for you on the kitchen table. It came this morning and I forgot to tell you about it. I put all the bills on the desk in the office."

The kitchen was off-limits to guests, and we—meaning Kelson, Aegis, and I—ate most of our meals at the kitchen table, which sat near the sliding glass doors leading out to the three-acre backyard. It gave us some privacy, and it was a way to delineate the family area from where the guests were allowed. The living room and parlor were also private. The French doors leading into both had very polite signs asking guests to please refrain from using the rooms. And of course, the butler's pantry, Kelson's room—which was downstairs—and the laundry room were private. There had been a grand ballroom in the massive mansion, and now it served as a combination library, games room, and sitting room for guests.

"Good afternoon," a voice came from behind me.

I jumped, startled. Turning around, I said with a laugh, "Franny, I've asked you before to stop doing that."

There, half in, half out of the wall, was Franny, our house ghost. She had been trapped here when I first bought the mansion, but a couple months ago I had managed to free her from the curse that held her here. But Franny decided to stay, using the house as a home base.

"I know, but it's so funny to watch you jump." She paused, then let out a laugh. "I went downtown today to look at all the sights. It's so beautiful out there. Bedlam has become such an incredibly pretty town over the years since I died."

When she was alive, Bedlam had barely been a blip on the island. But it had been founded by magical folk, even though Franny's family had been human. But they had been involved in spiritualism, or at least her father had.

"Yeah, *really* funny." But I couldn't help but smile. Franny had been annoying at first, but I had grown to like her, and I was grateful she had decided to stick around. "So what's happening in the spirit world? Anything interesting?"

"I was kind of hoping you'd ask that. I actually have a situation that I'd like to talk to you about."

I picked up the envelope from the table, frowning as I scanned the handwriting. It looked familiar, but I couldn't place it. I sat down at the table, easing myself into the chair so that my hip wouldn't complain. At least my curvy ass kept the bruising from hurting more than it would have if I had been thin. I started to open the envelope as I looked up at Franny.

"What's going on?"

"I found a ghost. A spirit."

"What do you mean, you *found* a ghost?" At that moment, Bubba came running up, followed by Luna. Bubba jumped up in my lap, landing hard on my thighs. He bounced up on the table, and Luna followed him. As I started to sputter, they made tracks off the table again, racing out of the kitchen. "Those two have got more energy than I think I ever had."

Bubba was a cjinn, basically a djinn in cat form. I had found him when he was a kitten, hundreds of years ago, when I had saved him from a burning barn. I wasn't sure what had happened to his mother or father, but on the way home he told me his name was Bubba, and he had been with me ever since. Cjinns were tricky. They had a wicked sense of humor, and if you rubbed their belly, they would often grant some secret wish you were harboring, although they might twist it for a little fun. Whenever Bubba rolled over on his belly, I warned my friends not to give him a tummy rub.

Luna had come to us when Bubba brought her home. I had found her owner, who was going to have her put down because she didn't want to deal with her anymore, so we had opened our home to her. Luna and Bubba loved each other. Given Bubba was fully cat, I was also grateful that I had Luna spayed. The last thing we needed were a dozen baby cjinns running around.

"What I mean is that I found a ghost out in the yard last night. He's confused. I want your permission to let him hang around for a while. I thought I might try to help him figure out who he was and what happened to him."

She sat down on the other side of the table. The problem was, she usually sat halfway through the chair so I could see it projecting inside of her. It was disconcerting, at best. Franny still wore the dress she had been wearing the day she died, a blue muslin gown with an ivory corset and an ivory shawl. She wore her hair up in a chignon, covered by a lace snood.

"What do you mean, *what happened to him?*" I set down the letter, not wanting to be rude.

"I mean, I want to help him find out what who he was and how he died. He has no clue of either answer. He's very lost, and he seems very nice."

I looked around, wondering if he was in the room with us now. Kelson was at the stove, Franny and I were at the table, and the only other one in the room at this point was

Lanyear, a barred owl who had become my familiar. He had been a gift from Arianrhod, the goddess our coven worshiped.

Lanyear gazed down from his perch in the corner of the room, near the ceiling. Aegis had built it for him, where neither cat could get to it.

"Is he here now? You didn't bring him in without permission, did you?" While I applauded Franny's philanthropic nature, I wasn't comfortable letting her bring home any stray ghost. That was a good way of inviting a demon or poltergeist into the house.

"Of course not," she said. She primly folded her hands in her lap. "*Of course* I would ask your permission first. He's waiting out back."

I let out a sigh. The last thing I wanted was another ghost hanging out in the house. We were already overrun with guests and friends.

"Oh, Franny, I don't know. It just seems like we'd be asking for trouble." I paused, then finally said, "Look, he's not going to get cold, and it's not like he's hungry. For now, if you could ask him to stay outside, he's welcome to hang around as long as he doesn't cause any trouble." I leaned back in the chair, wishing I could cross my legs, but when I tried crossing my right leg over my left, my hip pulled something horrible. And when I tried the other way, it still hurt.

She clapped her hands. "Thank you! I'm going to go talk to him. Maybe I can jog his memory somehow. He had to have died on the island, don't you think? For him to be here?"

I shrugged. "I honestly don't know. I'm not an expert on ghosts. I'm an expert on magic, and that's quite different. Now, I'm sorry to cut this short, but I have things to do."

"Of course. I'm sorry to take up your time," Franny said, and I suspected I had hurt her feelings.

"Franny, I think it's wonderful what you're doing. But I really need to think. Don't take it personally."

"Of course not," she said, rolling her eyes as she walked through the wall and vanished.

"If I had a nickel for every time I offended her, I'd be rich. I like Franny," I said loudly in case she was still hanging around, listening, "but she takes offense so easily. Now, let me look at this letter, and I'll help you make dinner."

Kelson waved we away. "Don't worry about dinner. One of the interns is due here in a half an hour and she can help me."

"How are the interns working out?"

"Wonderfully. Neverfall has some talented students, and given how hungry some of them are for pocket change, they do their work. I'm going to put in a load of laundry in, so I'll be back in a moment." Kelton headed out of the kitchen.

Finally alone, I slit open the envelope and shook out the single page that was nestled inside. As I opened it, my heart sank. I recognized the handwriting, all right.

> My dear Maddy, I hope you're thinking of me because I'm thinking of you. I can't wait to see you again, to hold you in my arms and show you how much you mean to me. You're mine, Maddy. You belong to me. I won't let anyone stand in our way.

We're meant to be together, and I'll be with you soon. And then, we'll never be apart again.

As I stared at the cursive on the paper, my heart froze. Whoever had written these letters was trouble, and I could feel that trouble heading right in my direction. I shoved the letter back in the envelope and stuck it in my pocket. I was afraid to tell Aegis, but the thought that someone out there might be targeting him, wanting to get rid of him so they could get to me, made me realize that I had to tell him. There were no two ways about it. He had to know.

When Aegis came out of the basement, where he made his lair, I was waiting for him. He pulled me into his arms, giving me a long kiss.

Tall and muscled, Aegis had jet-black hair that fell down to his mid-back. His eyes were a deep brown, and when he was aroused or hungry, crimson rings formed around the irises. His pale skin was almost alabaster. At one time, he had been a servant of Apollo, until Apollo cast him out, turning him into one of the Fallen. But vampire or not, Aegis had a gentle side to him—a side that loved kittens, murder mysteries, and baking. He treated me like a goddess.

"I dreamt about you last night," Aegis said, nuzzling my neck.

I was hungry for him, since the past few weeks had been a dry spell, given my injuries. "Kiss me again."

He pressed his cool lips against my own warm ones. Aegis never made me feel *less* than—less than a woman, less than an intelligent thinking person, less than a successful business owner. He supported me and shored me up. I trusted him in a way that I didn't trust anyone, except for Sandy and Bubba.

He brushed my hair back away from my face, cupping my chin with his fingers. "You're so beautiful. Every night when I wake up, I give thanks that you're in my life."

As much as I reveled in the compliments and flattery, I couldn't help but snort. "All right, what did you do now?" But I laughed as I said it.

"Enough, wench. So what's for dinner?" Vampires could eat if they wanted to, though it was merely for pleasure. But Aegis liked to eat. Thanksgiving had been wonderful, thanks to his deft touch in the kitchen.

"Pot roast and your apple pie. By the way, Kelson wondered if you could throw together a batch of dinner rolls? We're eating at six, so you have about ninety minutes."

"Of course I can. How was today? How is your rib doing?"

"Fairly good, and sore. Sandy and I went out shopping for our trousseaus, and we picked out the flowers for the wedding. Oh, and Franny has brought home some stray ghost. She wants to know if he can hang around."

"Why?"

"So she can help him figure out who he was and how he died. I told her yes, but to keep him out in the garden. And remember I told you about the Santas brawling down on Main Street last week?"

Aegis rolled his eyes. "Yeah, I remember."

"Well, they were at it again. Sandy and I had a front-row seat. Delia had to break them up. I guess it's a turf war thing." I realized that I was out of energy. "Can you make me a mocha? I could really use the buzz. Three shots? Please?" I fluttered my eyes at him, and Aegis laughed.

"All right, one mocha coming up. What flavors?" He headed over toward the espresso machine as I returned to the table.

"Peppermint, if you would. That sounds good." I was dreading telling him about the letters, but I figured that I had better do it now, instead of putting it off. The longer I procrastinated, the harder it would be. "I need to talk to you about something."

"What's going on?" He began to pull my shots.

"When you finish my mocha, we can talk. Before you ask, it's nothing to do with you. You didn't do anything, and I'm not upset. I just… Something concerns me."

Aegis fixed my mocha, then took a seat next to me. As he waited, I pulled out the letter from my pocket, then retrieved the one from my purse and set them on the table in front of him.

"I received these over the past week and a half. One arrived today, the other a few days ago. At first, I thought it might be a joke, so I didn't say anything. But now I'm not sure what to think." I took a sip of the peppermint mocha, closing my eyes as the cool mint cut through the dark chocolate.

Aegis opened the letters, reading first one, then the other. As he skimmed them, crimson rings formed around his eyes and I could tell he was upset.

"Who the hell sent these?" He slammed them on the table.

"I have no idea. It seems to be someone I know, given what the last letter said. But I don't know what to think." I stared at the envelopes, trying to recall where I had seen the handwriting before, but the memory eluded me.

"You don't think it's Fata Morgana, is it? She was in love with you."

The thought hadn't even occurred to me. But it was true, Fata Morgana had been in love with me. She carried a torch for me, and had taken to the sea when I rejected her.

"I don't think so. When she left a few months ago, we were good. We parted on easy terms. Besides, she's turning into a goddess now. She's got enough on her hands to deal with." I bit my lip, trying to think of who else it could be. "Craig's dead, so it can't be him. And as far as I know, nobody else is carrying a torch for me."

I had no idea who my secret admirer was, but it was creepy as hell.

"If you get any more of these, show me immediately. I think you should talk to Delia. She can start a case file, just in case something happens." Aegis leaned back in his chair, crossing his arms over his chest. He was wearing black jeans and a black muscle shirt, and he looked absolutely delicious. I wanted to tear off his clothes, but any sudden movements brought more pain than pleasure.

Kelson entered the room at that moment. "Hey, Aegis! Can you make the rolls for me?"

Aegis grunted, then handed me back the letters. "Call Delia tonight." He turned to Kelson. "Sure, I'll get them started now."

I bit my lip, not wanting to bother the sheriff with something that was so nebulous at this point. "I'll talk to her tomorrow. Let her have the evening to rest. She swamped, given it's the holidays. By the way, a string of lights on the Yule tree on the grand tree went out. I need you to fix them, because I can't."

We had a massive Yule tree in the grand ballroom, and a private one in the living room. I had also splurged and bought a smaller one for the dining room. They were all gorgeous, decked out in glimmering gold and silver. One of them was themed with blue-and-white ornaments, another with red and gold, and the third with multicolored ornaments.

Aegis laughed. "Put it down on my honey-do list. I'll take care of it after I finish making the rolls." He headed over to the counter, where he put on his apron. As he pulled out the flour and yeast, I tucked both letters in my purse. Kelson was starting the roast in the pressure cooker, and the intern was due any minute. Feeling as though there were one too many cooks in the kitchen, I decided to head to the office, to take care of business for the day.

CHAPTER FOUR

The next morning, while I was in the office sorting out the ledger, Kelson appeared at the door.

"Ralph Greyhoof is here. He's asking to see you."

"That's just what I need," I said. Ralph and I were getting along better than before, but a visit with him still wasn't my favorite way to spend an hour.

I stood, wincing. I was wearing jeans and a turtleneck, with an underbust corset, but my rib cage still ached. Aegis and I had spent a good hour in my bed, doing everything we could without actually having sex. We managed, but I was frustrated, and tired of hurting. I just wanted to get back to normal, and back naked in Aegis's arms.

I headed for the living room, taking it slow. "After I'm done with Ralph, can you bring me the Ache Begone?"

Kelson laughed. "Get too active last night?" she teased.

"I wish. I just want this bruise to heal up. It's better than it was, though. Jordan told me that in about two weeks, I'll have full movement in my hip again. He's given me some physical therapy exercises to work it out. The rib has a while to go, though."

As I entered the living room, Ralph stood. He had acquired a lot in the way of manners ever since he started dating Ivy Vine, a wood nymph. She was whipping him into shape and I hoped the relationship would last.

"Ralph! It's so good to see you." I didn't mind exaggerating a little when it came to Ralph. He wasn't a *bad* person—or satyr, rather. He was just denser than a fence post, and too suspicious for his own good.

He was holding a gift-wrapped box, and he held it out to me, almost shyly. "I brought you an early wedding present. I hope you like it."

I blinked. This was the last thing I had expected. I eased myself onto the sofa next to him. He hadn't tried to come onto me for quite some time, so I felt comfortable sitting next to him.

"Are you still hurting?" he asked.

I nodded. "My rib isn't fully healed, and my hip is still bruised. Craig did a number on me. I don't mind telling you, I'm glad he's dead."

About six weeks ago, my ex had kidnapped me, intending to kill me. Franny had actually saved my life, in an odd set of circumstances. But she hadn't been able to keep Craig from kicking the shit out of me.

"If he was still alive, I'd go after him myself." Ralph's eyes glimmered. "Men who beat up women piss me off."

Most satyrs adored women, too much so in many cases. I had dated several of them, a couple centuries ago. Or, rather, Sandy, Fata Morgana, and I had spent an orgy-filled year with a group of satyrs and wood nymphs. In all the time we'd spent with them, I had never seen one satyr raise his hand toward any woman. And contrary to most mythology, the satyrs I knew had *never* assaulted women. They always tried their best to seduce, but none I knew had ever forced himself on a woman.

"Well, thank you. I appreciate the sentiment. So, what's this?" I held up the box.

"Maddy, we have such a checkered past. I just wanted you to know how happy I am for you and Aegis. This is from Ivy and me."

Touched, I pulled on the satin ribbon that was holding the box closed. The box was beautiful, with an embossed ivory pattern on it, and I decided I'd keep that as well. When I took the lid off, I couldn't help but gasp. Inside was a small painting, framed, of Aegis and me. A portrait of our faces together. I looked up at Ralph, not sure what to say.

"Do you like it?" he asked.

"Like it? *I love it*. When did you have this done? It's so beautiful, and they got Aegis's likeness perfect. Mine too, but I imagine you had a photograph to work off of for me."

He nodded. "I'm so glad you like it. Yes, I gave them a photo of you that I took sometime back. And don't give me *that* look—I took the picture before I met Ivy. I asked the painter to go with me to a show that Aegis's band played. Remember the gig before Thanksgiving? Anyway, Umber drew a few sketches while we were there, and he worked off of those. Do you think Aegis will like it?"

"I *know* he will. Ralph, this is one of the most thoughtful gifts I've ever received. Thank you so much." I paused for a moment, then let out a sigh. "I'm sorry we got off to a rocky start when I moved to Bedlam. I hope you understand that I'm not trying to steal your guests."

He shrugged, but gave me a nod. "Yeah, I do. And I'm sorry for my part in everything. I have a short fuse." He paused, then asked, "Can I ask you a question, Maddy? And I want an honest answer."

"That's loaded. All right. I'll do my best, if it's something I'm willing to answer—or can."

"Do you think that Ivy and I have a chance to make it? Long term, I mean?" He sounded so sincere I couldn't help but feel sorry for him. Satyrs looking for a monogamous relationship were fighting an uphill battle. Their sexuality was like a loaded gun, ready to go off at any time.

"Well, some of your people manage it. I think, if you really want it to work, and if Ivy really wants the relationship to work, then there's always a chance you can make it. So much depends on what you're willing to compromise on, and what your definition of 'long term' is."

"What do you mean?"

"Take Aegis and me. We're getting married. We love each other…so much that I can't even fathom being apart. But neither one of us will *ever* commit *till death do us part*. I'll live for hundreds of years—I'm headed toward four hundred as it is. Aegis has been alive for over two millennia. We're bound to live a lot longer, unless something unexpected happens. What if we can't keep those promises? Neither one of us wants to make an oath that we might have to break some time in the future."

"So what will you pledge?" Ralph asked.

"We've talked it over and decided that we're going to commit to each other as long as love shall last. That's an honest assessment of what we can promise, and we'll do our best to make our love last as long as we can. But whether we're together for ten years or a hundred, or even a thousand, the fact is we love each other right now and we want to be together."

Ralph thought about that for a while. "That makes a lot of sense. Ivy's been hinting around about wanting more of a commitment. I'm not about to get married at this point, but I've considered offering her a promise ring. What do you think?"

I wasn't surprised. Ivy had practically taken over every aspect of Ralph's life except for the inn, and while he had improved for the better, I wonder how long it could last. While I wasn't about to encourage Ralph to return to his former behavior, the fact was, I wasn't sure just how healthy it was for him to sublimate his entire life to her.

"I want to ask you something, Ralph. You don't have to answer me, now or ever. I just want you to think about this for a while. Are you really happy? I know you love Ivy, but do you like who you are when you're around her?" I paused, biting my lip. "I think when you've answered that, you'll know whether or not you should give her a ring."

Ralph gazed into my eyes, and for a moment I thought he was about to cry. But he just sighed, and looked away.

After a moment he turned back to me. "Sometimes you're too perceptive, Maddy. I'm not going to answer you. But you're forcing me to think about things that I have swept under the rug. Let me ask *you* a question. How do you keep changes that you like in yourself, when you don't have somebody flogging you to stay that way? In other words, without somebody on my back, how do I make certain that I'm able to keep the changes that I like?"

Ralph had answered my question, whether or not he realized it.

"I guess it depends on how much you want to change. Habits are hard to break, especially the ones that aren't good for us. I suppose the answer is you remind yourself how important the changes are. You set yourself up a reminder system, or maybe even something to motivate you. You know, dangle a carrot in front of your nose." I paused as he stared at me. In that moment, I saw the vulnerable side of Ralph.

"Look, Ralph. Nobody can make you a better person, except for you. If it doesn't come from inside, then nothing you can do will make those changes stick. If you really like some of the changes that you've made while you've been with Ivy, then you have to decide how much they mean to you. Because what happens if she decides to leave you? Are you going to just throw everything to the wind?"

I could practically see the wheels turning in his head as he held out his hand. I took it, and he raised my fingers to his lips, kissing them gently and then letting go as he stood.

"Thank you, Maddy. I'm going to say this once, and I don't want you to say anything. You said that the painting was one of the most thoughtful gifts you've ever received. I just want you to know that over the past few months you've given me a lot of advice. I couldn't receive any greater gift than that. And now, I'm going to go home and have a long discussion with Ivy after I think through what

I want to say." He laughed, winking at me. "See? I'm trying to think about what traits I want to keep."

And on that note, Ralph headed toward the door. "Don't bother seeing me out. I can find my way. You rest that rib. You want to be in good shape for your wedding."

As I heard the front door close behind him, I sat back against the sofa, thinking about our conversation. Ralph was making headway. Given the loutish oaf he had been when I first moved to Bedlam over a year ago, that was saying something. Yawning, I picked up a magazine off the table, but at that moment my phone rang. I dropped the magazine and pulled out my phone, glancing at caller ID. It was Delia.

"Hey, what's up?" I asked, hitting the speaker button.

"Maddy, I have a problem and I wondered if you could help." She sounded frazzled. A little frantic, actually. "I know you still hurt, and if you say no, that's fine."

"What's wrong? Are you having problems with the Santas again?"

"No, actually, it's something entirely different and I'm not sure what to do about it. I'm downtown near the town square. A group of gnomes landed right near the fountain. There are ten of them, and they're extremely confused." She cleared her throat.

"Gnomes? You're *not* talking about the red-capped little creatures out of children's books, are you?"

Gnomes actually existed, but not the way most humans saw them or portrayed them. They weren't tiny little people with red hats and jolly personalities. Gnomes were actually a form of forest Fae, and they could be quite terrifying when angered. They were small, and they did wear toadstools as hats, but they had very little to do with humans. They were mostly around to help wounded animals inside of the woodlands.

"Yeah, I'm talking about the *storybook* gnomes." She paused. "Do you remember when Snow White showed up last year?"

"Of course I do. That was Ralph's fault. He's the one who gated her out of the fairytale and tried to stick her and her dwarves in a raunchy porn movie." Yeah, Ralph *had* changed for the better.

"Well, *somebody* brought these gnomes out of some book or TV show. They have no clue of what they're doing here, or why. I'm trying to round them up, but they're racing around like a pack of puppies on espresso. They won't talk to me other than to ask, 'Where are we? Who are you? Why are we here?' And every time I try to round them up, they manage to slip out of my hands. I hate to sound crude, but it's like trying to run down a pack of greased piglets."

"Piglets and puppies, that sounds delightful. All right, where are you exactly?"

"Near McGee's pharmacy. You'll come down right away?"

"On my way. Let me just grab a latte." I pocketed my phone. Yeah, this was just another day in Bedlam.

CHAPTER FIVE

The city streets were filled with bustling throngs of shoppers. Bedlam's town square had a fountain in the center of it, and during the warmer months the water streamed up, shifting colors through the spectrum of the rainbow.

Near the town square was the central park, where most of the community events were held. A roundabout guided cars to circle the central fountain, slowing traffic so that no one could speed through the center of town.

I parked in one of the parking slots across the street. Delia was in the center of the square, next to the fountain. From here, I could also see the gnomes. They were around two feet tall and their red hats glittered in the fluttering snow. I zipped up my jacket and using my cane for balance, I cautiously made my way across the slippery crosswalk. If someone wanted to run me over, that was their problem.

A smile of relief spread across Delia's face when she saw me.

"Thank gods you're here. I'm about at my wits' end. This is the fourth bizarre call we've had today." She wiped her forehead.

"Are you feeling okay?" I asked, ignoring the gnomes for a moment.

They were gathered on the concrete bench that ran around the fountain, chattering to each other in a language I couldn't understand. Two of them were arguing so loudly that I expected a fistfight to break out any moment.

Delia shrugged. "I don't know, to tell you the truth. I'm just so tired of all these weird incidents. This morning, old Mrs. Nassau was caught *streaking* in the snow in front of Temples Assisted Living Facility. At dawn, there was a major row over at the East Coast Marina. Your friend Gillymack decided to borrow a kayak without paying for it. Ryan, of Ryan's Kayak Rental, caught him. Gillymack is now in jail, with a broken nose and a broken arm. And Ryan is in jail for assault."

"Wow. You *have* had a busy morning." I glanced at the gnomes.

"Oh, I'm not done. Not in the least. Let me see," she said, shaking her head. "Myrtle Woods had a meltdown when somebody chopped down her holly tree. Considering she's one of the Winter Fae, and that holly tree is sacred to her, she's threatening bodily harm if she finds out who did it."

I groaned, easing myself onto the edge of the fountain. "Anything else?"

"Hmm, is there anything? No, I guess not, unless you count the call I received from Auntie Tautau. She warned me that something is askew in the web surrounding

Bedlam. She said that the energy's shifted and chaos is flooding the island. She's not sure what's going on, but she wanted to give me a heads-up."

As Delia finished talking, she slumped back against the bench next to the gnomes and crossed her arms. She let out an exhausted sound, and looked up at me.

"If Auntie Tautau called you, then there's something seriously askew."

The Aunties were a group of incredibly powerful witches. Nobody was sure what race they were, although they looked human enough. They were ancient, irreverent, sometimes raunchy, and they belonged to no group, coven, or organization. Sometimes they worked with the Society Magicka, and I knew that Auntie Tautau also worked with the WPP, the Witches' Protection Program. But other than that, nobody knew where they came from, or who they answered to.

"I'd appreciate it if you would talk to her, if you can. If she's home. She does have a way of disappearing when she doesn't want company. Anyway, what about the gnomes?"

"Let's see what I can do." I walked over and took a seat on the other side of the gnomes.

They stopped what they were doing and stared at me suspiciously. The two gnomes on the brink of an argument also paused. Finally, one of the gnomes—a stout little man with ruddy cheeks and a bright red nose—sauntered toward me, hands on his hips. He let out a loud belch and I could smell whiskey on his breath.

"Are you in charge?" His voice seemed way too loud for his size.

"In a way. Who are you?"

"Digger," he said. "And who are you, sweet cheeks?"

I suppressed the desire to knock him over. "Address me like that again and I'll toss you in the fountain. I'm Maudlin Gallowglass, and I'm the High Priestess of the Moonrise Coven. Where are you from? And how did you get here?"

"That's the same thing the sheriff asked. And I'll tell you what we told her. We were in Summer Rise, and the next minute, we were here. We were hiking up to Mount Jubilee."

Even though he smelled like he'd bathed in booze, he sounded as sober as I was. But something he said rang a bell. I closed my eyes, trying to remember where I had heard of Mount Jubilee. Then, I knew.

"Hold on a second." I pulled out my phone, and pulled up my E-reader app. I thumbed through the library until I came to a book. Sure enough, the title was *The Tales Of Summer Rise*. I opened the book and skimmed through until I found a story titled "Digger's Big Adventure on Mount Jubilee."

"Delia, can I talk to you in private?"

She followed me far enough away so the gnomes couldn't hear us.

I showed her my phone. "Summer Rise is a town in a kids' book. These gnomes are straight out of the book. So the question is, who gated them in?" I stared at the children's book, frowning. "It wasn't Ralph. I'm sure of it. He's kept his nose clean lately, thanks to Ivy."

"Well, if Ralph didn't bring them here, who did? And why?" She glanced over her shoulder. "What do I do with them?"

I wasn't going to take them home, that was for sure. I'd

made that mistake with Snow White and things had turned into one big mess. "Find them a hotel?"

"There are ten men on the fountain who can barely scramble up on a stepstool, let alone a bed or sofa. A hotel room would be useless. A bed would be like a football field."

I tried to think. If we asked Sandy, she'd do it, but Mr. Peabody, her skunk, would probably terrorize the poor gnomes. Ralph and his brothers were out of the question. And just about everybody else that I knew wouldn't have the right facilities to help the gnomes manage.

"I guess we'll have to ask Sandy. Her assistant, Alex, can rig up something. Let me call her."

When Sandy answered, she was breathing hard. I could hear a whir in the background that told me she was on her treadmill. She took three yoga classes a week, four cardio classes, and she met with her personal trainer twice a week to lift weights. I had tried to join her for a while, but I just wasn't cut out for that level of exercise.

"Hey Sandy, do you have a room that we can store some gnomes in?"

She paused, then sputtered. "Who's got gnome trouble?"

"Delia. Somehow, ten gnomes were transported out of a storybook and ended up in the town square. We're talking the red-capped little men, not forest gnomes. They don't know how they got here and we have no idea of what to do with them. But we need a safe place to keep them until we can figure out how to send them back."

"This isn't Ralph's fault, is it?" Sandy asked suspiciously. She had been right by my side during the whole Snow White incident.

"I don't think so." I paused, then added, "I got another letter, by the way."

"Have you told Aegis yet?"

"Yes, I showed him the letters. He asked if I thought it might be Fata Morgana, but I told him no. For one thing, if she went off the deep end I think we'd know it in a big way."

"You're probably right. I don't think it's her, either. But who is behind it? Craig's dead. Do you have any other unrequited crushes?"

" I have no clue. But back to the gnomes. Do you have room in your house to fix up a space for them?"

"If they'll accept being locked in a room. I'm not about to let them roam free around my house. Bring them over when you're ready. I'll have Alex prepare a space for them." And with that, she signed off.

"Sandy says bring the gnomes over to her place. How are you going to round them up?" I kept my voice low as I stared at the gnomes.

"I have no clue. What kind of carrots do gnomes like? Gnome women? Food? I have no clue," Delia said.

"I know what they'll jump at. Leave it to me." I strode over to the gnomes, wincing as my hip twinged. "Hey, fellows? How would you like some ale?" My hunch was correct. They turned as one, staring at me with hungry looks.

"You got food, too?" one of them asked.

I nodded. "Plenty of it. So, up for a ride?" I pointed to one of the passing cars. "Have you ever been in a car before?"

They shook their heads.

I turned Delia. "Maybe you should take them in the

back of the squad car." It occurred to me that even storybook gnomes weren't very nice. They seemed to fight a lot.

Delia slowly pulled the patrol car up to the curb, got out, and opened the back door. The gnomes started to argue who was getting in first.

"All right, knock it off with the fighting!" I shouted.

The gnomes stopped their bickering and turned to stare at me.

"We're taking you somewhere safe where you can eat and drink. And then we'll try to figure out how to send you back to where you came from. But you have to promise to behave. *No fighting*, understand? And no messing about with stuff that's none of your business."

One by one, the gnomes agreed, grumbling all the while. When Delia went to pick one up, though, he smacked her hand.

"Let her do it." He pointed to me. "The one with the boobs."

Rolling her eyes, Delia stepped back, making way for me. I lifted the gnomes, one at a time, and placed them in the back seat, shutting the door so they couldn't scramble out again.

Finally, I was finished. "Sandy will be waiting. Alex is there and he'll help."

At that moment, sounds of a shouting match interrupted me. We turned around, looking into the crowd, only to see two women going at it in front of one of the department stores. They were next to an outdoor sales table. It looked as though one had found a scarf she liked and the other had grabbed hold of the other end. They were playing tug-of-war with it, while the shopkeeper was yelling at them to stop.

With an irritated look, Delia pushed through the crowd. "Break it up! Seriously, what the hell are you fighting about, Madge?"

I recognized Madge Henney on one end of the scarf. The other woman, I didn't know.

"Can't you make them stop? They're ruining my merchandise," the shopkeeper said.

"Hold your horses. I'll do what I can." Delia took hold of the scarf, yanking it out of both women's hands. "Act your age! You're adult women and not a couple of whining teenagers. You're fighting over a stupid scarf that isn't even that attractive. What started it?"

Madge Henney stared at the ground, her face flushing. "I don't know. I just wanted it and she grabbed it out of my hands."

"I did not! I saw it before you did."

Thoroughly disgusted, Delia handed the scarf back to the store manager.

"They stretched it out! Who's going to pay for this?" the clerk said.

"Why don't you bill them both, and each can pay half of the cost." She glared at the women. "And they *will* pay it, won't they?"

As the women grudgingly nodded, Delia let out an exasperated sigh. "I've got to go. And I don't want to have to come back here, you understand?" Once again, she turned to Madge and the other woman. Again they both nodded. Delia made her way back through the crowd to me. She gave me a long, frustrated look.

"Some days, this job is just not worth it. I'm heading

over to Sandy's. Do you want to meet me there?" I could tell she was hoping I'd say yes, but the truth was, I had no interest in dealing with a group of rowdy gnomes.

"Sorry," I said with a grin. "I have other things to do. But I'll check on how they are later today, and I'll start trying to figure out how they got here. I'll call Auntie Tautau and see if she'll talk to me." With that, I hightailed it back to my rented sedan before Delia could ask me for another favor.

CHAPTER SIX

By the time I got home, I was exhausted—more sore than tired. I glanced at the clock, and saw that it was almost four. That meant Aegis would wake up in another twenty minutes. I slumped down at the table, wanting nothing more than a long massage and a hot bath.

"You look like something the cat dragged in," Kelson said, setting a tall mug of mocha in front of me, along with a plate of chocolate chip cookies.

"Bless you," I said, taking a sip. I wiped the whipped cream off my lips, grateful as the warmth slid down my throat. "I love the holidays, but why do they always seem so stressful? I just realized I haven't finished my shopping, and I'm usually on top of things like that."

"You're not just celebrating the holidays. The bed-and-breakfast is full, *and* you're planning a wedding." Kelson sat across from me, a cup of tea in hand. "Don't beat yourself up. Craig already did that for you. Your body's still recuperating and you have every reason to be tired."

I stifled a yawn. Finally, I attempted a very small stretch, grimacing as the pain hit. After another yawn, I picked up one of the cookies and bit into it.

"How's everybody doing today? I wish I had time to be a better hostess."

"Nobody's complaining, and everybody seems to be out and about a lot. Except, of course, Henry. And he's keeping to himself. He seems to be in a reclusive mood lately. Ever since he and Franny had that blowup, I think they've been trying to avoid each other."

Henry Mosswood was a semi-permanent resident at the Bewitching Bedlam. He was writing the history of Bedlam, although I had my doubts whether he would actually manage to finish the book. He'd been cursed long ago when he had broken the heart of a witch. She had hexed him to live an extremely long life but to never find love. When Franny had developed a crush on him and thought he reciprocated her feelings, things had become tense. Now, Henry kept to his room and the two seldom spoke.

"That was an unfortunate incident. I do blame him for leading her on. He's old enough to know how women take things." By now I had eaten five of the cookies and I pushed the plate away. "Take this away or I'll eat all of them."

"And that's a problem?" Kelson asked, picking up the plate and returning it to the counter.

"If I want to fit my wedding dress, it's a problem. Otherwise I wouldn't care. But it's too late to do any more adjustments on the dress, and I've been stress-eating too much."

The door to the basement opened and Aegis entered the room.

Every time I looked at him, the world became a little bit brighter.

"Good evening, love," he said, leaning down to give me a long kiss.

I sighed, melting into his arms. "It's been a day, I'll tell you that." I gazed into his eyes. At one time I would have killed him without question, without knowing anything about his life before he was turned.

"Oh, my Maddy. I'm sorry. I wish you didn't hurt," he whispered. "I'd take you up to your bed and make love to every inch of you. But for now, we'll settle for kisses and cuddles until you heal. Come on, let's eat an early dinner." Aegis kissed me again. "What's on the menu tonight?"

"Lasagna," Kelson said from over by the oven. "But it won't be ready for ninety minutes. I can make you something simple, if you like."

I thought about it, then shook my head. "We'll wait for the lasagna."

While Kelson made the salad and assigned the intern who was helping her to set the main dining table for all our guests, I told Aegis about what had happened with the gnomes.

"Have you tried to call Auntie Tautau yet?" he asked.

I shook my head. "I suppose I should." I pulled out my phone and called her number, but I got voice mail, asking me to leave a message. Ten to one, she was screening, but I went ahead and asked her to call me when she got the chance.

Aegis and I went into the office and looked over the

books while waiting for Kelson to call us to dinner, and by the time we were done, I was even more grateful I had waited for the lasagna because it was perfect. As we passed by the dining table, going into the kitchen to eat, it seemed that all our guests, including Henry, were eating in again. I waved to them, leaving them to talk among themselves, and Aegis and I closed the door between the dining room and the kitchen to give ourselves some privacy.

I sat at the table while he brought over our plates, thinking how lucky I was. I might be injured, but I had a man who treated me like a queen, I owned a beautiful old bed-and-breakfast, I had wonderful friends, and I had a cjinn who was my closest buddy. Life was good.

"What is it?" Aegis asked as he sat down next to me.

"I was just thinking how much I have to be grateful for," I said, picking up my fork and digging in. The lasagna was hot and full of flavor, the salad, cool and crisp, and the pie tasted like a cool autumn night by the fire.

"That's always a good thing to do." Kelson carried the pie into the living room on a tray. When she returned, her tray full of dishes, she set them down, dished up a plate for herself, and joined us. "I'm so tired. Even with the interns, this many guests on a regular basis is taxing."

I winced. "I'm sorry. I wish I could help out more."

"I saw the baskets sitting next to the laundry room. I can wash all the sheets tonight while you're asleep," Aegis said.

Kelson wiped a stray hair back from her forehead where it had gotten loose from her braid. "Thank you. I was busy cooking all day, and Sera and Jeff—the interns—

were cleaning, and shoveling snow so the guests can get their cars out of the driveway."

We ate in a comfortable silence, the food creating a cushion against all of the outside problems. By the time we finished our pie, I leaned back and smiled, patting my stomach.

"Good food goes a long ways, doesn't it?"

Aegis nodded. "Yeah, it's one of life's joys—"

My phone jangled, cutting him off. It was Sandy's ringtone.

A sudden premonition swept over me, and I sobered. "Hey, what's up?"

"Maddy, Jenna's gone. The school called. She missed her Magickal Chants class this afternoon. Her roommate Lara thought she might be cutting class, but when Jenna didn't show up for dinner, Lara got worried and went to the RA. They're searching the school and grounds right now." Sandy's voice trembled. She had gone from unsure guardian to doting mother over the past months.

I frowned. "Could she be on her way home? Maybe she decided to come visit you and got on the wrong bus. Did you call her phone?"

"Yes, and so did the school. It just goes straight to voice mail. She's disabled her Find Friends app. I don't know what to do."

I thought back to what she had told me earlier. "You said you were worried that Jenna's hanging around with a bad crowd. Could she be with them?"

Sandy hesitated for a moment. "Maybe. I wish I could remember the names of those kids. Maybe Lara knows. I know I'm asking a lot, but could you go with me to

Neverfall? I don't want to go alone. Somebody needs to be here in case she shows up, so Max is staying home."

Saying no never even crossed my mind. "Of course I'll come with you. Aegis can drive me over and he can hang with Max while you and I go out to the school."

"Thanks, Maddy." She sniffled. "I don't know what I'd do if something's happened to her."

I set my phone on the table and turned to Aegis. "Jenna's missing. Sandy wants me to go with her to Neverfall and of course I said I would. Do you mind hanging out with Max?"

Aegis immediately jumped out of his seat. "I'll get our coats. Kelson, can you hold down the fort here?"

"Of course. You just do whatever you need to do," she said.

"If Jenna shows up here, lock her up. Don't let her get away. And call me." I accepted my jacket from Aegis, letting him help me on with it, snugging the front closed.

"I'll keep her here if she shows up," Kelson said.

I kicked off my slippers and carefully zipped up my boots, ignoring the twinges. "Come on, let's hit the road," I said, handing my purse to Aegis.

He led the way to the car. I glanced up into the night sky. The sky had cleared and the temperature was down to thirty-four already. The stars glimmered as the smell of woodsmoke filled the air. As I stared at the sky, I breathed a quick prayer to Arianrhod that Jenna would show up safely.

CHAPTER SEVEN

By the time we got to Sandy's, she was in a state. She was pacing in the spacious kitchen of her mansion, her boots beating out a steady rhythm on the polished tile floor. Max sat on one of the bar stools at the counter. As we entered the room, Sandy ran over to me and threw her arms around my shoulders, crying. I let out a shriek as my rib protested. With a chagrined look on her face, she immediately pulled back.

"I'm so sorry. Are you okay?" By the look on her face, she felt worse than I did.

"Don't worry about it. I'll be all right. Aegis is going to stay with Max while you and I go up to the school. Are you sure you can drive?"

She nodded. "No problems there." She turned back to Max. "We'll be back pretty soon. Call me if she shows up. Call me if anybody sees her. Call me—"

"I'll call you if *anything* happens. Don't you worry about that." Max Davenport was a big bear of a man. Or rather—tiger. A tiger-shifter, he was tall and muscled, with hair the color of wheat, and dark brown eyes. He was wearing a pair of dark blue jeans, and a cable knit sweater.

With Sandy carrying my purse, we headed out to her sedan. She tucked me in the passenger seat and we were on the way.

"This isn't like her, Maddy. This isn't like Jenna at all. Even though she's been running around with the crowd I don't approve of, she always returns my calls. And she never cuts class. She loves school too much."

I didn't want to add to her worries, but Jenna was reaching that rebellious age, and kids didn't always act like themselves. While Jenna had a good head on her shoulders and a lot of common sense, she was still subject to peer pressure. But I couldn't say that—not right at this moment.

"Did you let the headmaster know were coming?"

"I did. Leroy is waiting for us."

Leroy Jerome was a tall, handsome man with skin as dark as the night. He was the headmaster of the Neverfall Academy for Gifted Students, a school for magically gifted students from kindergarten through twelfth grade. The academy sat on over a thousand acres on the northeastern side of the island. It was set out on a cliff, overlooking the water, and it was founded when the island was first settled by the Pretcom, around two hundred years ago.

Sandy fell silent as we drove through the darkening evening. We followed the curving shoreline, the road ascending as we headed northeast. Within fifteen minutes, we were well above the water and the guard rail was covered with reflectors as we entered a series of S-curves.

The academy was on a spit overlooking the ocean, the turnoff on the left, or inland side of the island. The drive leading to the school was spacious, and the campus was covered with trees. We slowed as we approached the main gates.

Rather than drive into one of the parking lots, Sandy parked in one of the visitors' spaces near the main campus. I had brought my temporarily disabled placard and hung on the rearview mirror. Walking any distance with my injuries hurt like hell. As we stepped out of the car, a fresh flurry of snow came tumbling down. I prayed that they had shoveled the walkway. The last thing I needed was to fall.

As we made our way to the administrative offices, Sandy glanced over at me. "I'm so sorry, Maddy. I should have thought about your injuries before I asked you to come with me. Are you okay?"

While the cold and exertion was making me ache, I didn't want to tell her that. I shook my head. "It's not too bad. Don't worry about it. Just don't walk too fast and I'll be okay."

The buildings of Neverfall were old stone. The entire campus echoed with magic, and the stones themselves sang out, low and humming, almost out of earshot. It was the song of energy, the music of the spheres. It was comforting, and enveloped us like a shroud of mist.

We entered the main admin building and about one hundred yards before the double doors that led to the cafeteria, we took a left. A moment later we entered the headmaster's office. The secretary took one look at us and waved us back toward his office.

"He's waiting for you. Go on in," she said.

The headmaster was studying a file folder. As we entered the room, he tossed the file folder to one side and stood, leaning forward to shake hands. He nodded for us to take a seat in the leather wingback chairs opposite his desk.

Leroy Jerome was a shadow witch. While most witches worked with one particular element, shadow witches worked out on the astral. They were very powerful and also very rare. Sandy and I had speculated that Jenna might end up a shadow witch once she found her affinity, but there was no way of knowing until she was tested. And the school couldn't do that until she was fifteen. It simply wasn't safe to put her through the tests before then.

"I understand that you're concerned about Jenna," Leroy said. "I'll cut right to the chase. I've had security out looking for her. The last time she was seen was right before lunch. She told her roommate Lara that she wouldn't be in the cafeteria. She said she was going out for a walk to try and solve some sort of problems she was having. Then she didn't show up for any of her afternoon classes."

"I hate to bring this up, because I was hoping it would resolve itself," Sandy said. "But Jenna's been running with a crowd I don't approve of. I've tried not to interfere too much because I've been afraid that my objections might push her toward them. I'm not sure what the group's name is, but it's some sort of underground group here at Neverfall."

"I know the group," Leroy said. "They call themselves the Makers, and while they *seem* unsavory, when you get down to the core, they're pretty much just a bunch of kids trying to rebel in the ways they can think of. They've never caused any real harm—mostly they're emo and angsty—and they feel like they don't belong in the system. But who among us never felt that way? We all thought we were invincible at one time, and we all felt that nobody listened to us. I wouldn't worry too much about her friends unless you catch her doing something that you really don't approve of." He leaned back in his chair, frowning.

"What do they do?" I asked.

"Oh, they try a bit of spell work that's above their level, usually nothing dangerous. They act like they're too good for studying, but none of them have failing grades. If I thought any of them was bullying a student, I'd put an end to it. But you have to give teens some leeway, and you have to let them burn their fingers now and then."

Sandy looked stricken. "So she's been missing since lunch? Have you got anyone searching the grounds? Maybe she fell and hurt herself."

"I have every available security officer out looking for her, as well as a group of volunteers from our search and rescue class. If she's on the grounds of Neverfall, we will find her. But Jenna's pretty resourceful. I wouldn't worry just yet. Chances are she'll come home before midnight, with some plausible excuse."

Sandy slowly stood. "Please call if you hear anything. And if she shows up, keep her here till I can pick her up."

I followed her out the door, suddenly remembering that Leroy had once asked me if I was serious with Aegis.

I liked the man, and if I wasn't with my hot vampire, I would have probably gone out with him. I paused, suddenly wondering if he could be behind the letters. But his energy was clear, and he was too smart to approach me that way. I glanced back at him, but he just shot me a smile and went back to his work.

On the way out the front door, Sandy burst into tears. "What if she's…"

"Shut up. She's fine. We'll find her and bring her home. Trust me." And with that, we headed back to the car.

On the way back to Sandy's house, I asked her, "Have you called Delia yet?"

She shook her head. "I was going to call as soon as we got home. I wanted to make sure that Leroy had done everything he could to find her first."

"Why don't I give her a call while we're on the way? She can meet us at your house." I placed the call.

As I got off the phone, Sandy said, "This makes it real."

"What do you mean?"

"Calling the cops is always the final step. It's that moment when you acknowledge that something is desperately wrong, and that it's not going to fix itself. I was hoping Jenna would be there waiting in Leroy's office. I kept thinking they'd find her, and she would be sitting there, waiting for me. I know it's stupid. They would have called if they had found her. But you know how the mind can work."

"Yeah, I understand."

When I had been married to Craig, my ex, I kept

hoping that he would wake up one day and realize how poorly he was treating me. But that day had never come, and when I finally screwed up the courage to leave him, I realized that I had been staying out of humiliation.

"What are you thinking of?" Sandy asked.

"Craig. How I spent ten years with a man who stopped loving me after the first six months. I spent ten years taking his bullshit and never speaking up because I was afraid to admit that our marriage was a failure. I wanted him to change. I wanted him to be the good guy I first thought he was. And that was never going to happen. You tried to tell me, but I was in too deep to listen."

"You're being too hard on yourself," she said. "I don't care whether you're a witch or a shifter or human, when somebody constantly tells you that you're worthless, after a while you believe them. When you pulled away from me I wanted to beat Craig into a pulp, but I knew that you had to be ready to leave. I'm glad he's dead, Maddy. You don't know how much I hated that man for what he did to you."

A rush of warmth flooded through me. Sandy had been there for me from the beginning. We had gone to hell and back together, along with Fata Morgana. Only somewhere along the way we had lost her. And even though we had reunited recently, she would never be ours again, not the way she was in the beginning.

"I want Fata at our wedding. I want her there because she *belongs* there. Do you think Auntie Tautau might be able to find her for us?"

"I don't know, but we can ask her. I wish we could go ask her about Jenna, but I have a feeling she'll tell us it was too soon." Sandy's voice was trembling and she clutched the steering wheel like it was a lifeline.

"Does Jenna have a boyfriend?"

She shook her head. "I know she dates a little, because she always asks my permission if she can go out with a boy. But no one boy in particular. She's dated three boys in the past two months. There was Ryan, and Kenneth, and a boy named Dexter. They all seemed nice. I insisted on meeting them before I allowed her to go out with them. I didn't get any bad feelings about any of them."

None of the names rang alarm bells for me either. As I eased into her driveway, parking as close to the house as I could, Delia pulled in next to us.

"Well, let's get this over with," Sandy said. "I suppose the next step is to call out search and rescue island-wide." And with that, she stepped out of the car, her expression as bleak as her words.

CHAPTER EIGHT

We gathered in Sandy's parlor, where Max had built a huge fire in the massive stone fireplace. Double-sided, the fireplace divided the dining room from the parlor. Aegis handed out wine, except for Delia, who shook her head. As the smooth flavors of raspberry and cinnamon trickled down my throat, I leaned back, trying to relax.

Sandy told Delia everything that had happened, and what Leroy had said. "I know the cops always say that kids just wander off, but Jenna's not that kind of girl."

Delia held up her hand. "Don't protest. I'm not going to blow this off. I know what kind of girl Jenna is, and I can't see her running away, or just ditching school and not checking in later with friends. Do you know what was on her mind?"

"No." Sandy shook her head. "Jenna's been a little rebellious lately, that I will say. She's entering that stage that all teenagers go through where they don't want their parents to know everything. I think if I were still just her guardian and not her adoptive mother now, she might have talked to me more. But that dynamic has changed."

"I'll put out an APB on her. Derek can call out the Majestic Mountain Squad. He'll scramble everyone and get them looking for her. I'll also send someone down to the ferry landing to see if she took the ferry. They usually don't let kids go alone without a permission slip from their parents."

She paused and cleared her throat. "I have to tell you, something is happening in this town. The past couple days have been incredibly violent."

"Was there another fight?" I asked.

Delia nodded. "Not only was there a fight, but this time someone died."

I stared at her. "You're kidding. Anybody we know?"

"I don't know if you knew him. His name was Forrest and he was a member of the Summer Fae. He didn't hang around downtown much, mostly near Cliffside Park."

I shook my head. The name didn't ring a bell. "What happened? I don't think I've met him."

"What happened is old man Tucker, who runs a stall at the Winter Carnival, beat him to death with a tire iron when Forrest tried to steal one of his handmade recorders." Delia looked shell-shocked.

Aegis let out a slow whistle. "He beat him to death over a *recorder*? Was it made of gold?"

Delia shook her head. "I know. It seems insane, doesn't it? To kill someone over a twenty-dollar musical instrument? That's ridiculous."

"Did he say why he did it? And even more important, have you caught him yet?" I asked.

"Oh, he admitted to it. Tucker also says he doesn't know why he did it. He said when Forrest picked one of his recorders and started to walk away with it, he saw red and just went postal on him. The closest thing he could grab as a weapon was a tire iron that he'd been meaning to lend to a friend who needed to pry open a trunk. We've grilled him, but he's sticking to his story. In fact, he turned himself into the police when he realized what he'd done. He said that it was like this pressure inside that boiled over, and he lost it."

"That's a freaking scary thing," Max said. "Suppose that had been a child. Would he have done the same thing?"

Sandy met out a little cry, raising her hand to her lips. "Do you think he found Jenna? Do you think he found her and killed her for some reason?"

"No, I do *not*. But I'd like to know what the hell is going on. There's something happening to this town. We've had a rash of incidents lately, like the brawling Santas and so forth. I really want to know what Auntie Tautau thinks about it."

"I called her and left a message, but she hasn't called me back yet." Which wasn't surprising, given the Aunties worked on their own timelines, and would not be pressured.

While Delia called Derek to activate the search and rescue, Aegis disappeared into the kitchen and began to make sandwiches. I suspected that Sandy hadn't eaten anything for several hours. And she wouldn't eat unless we ate with her, so when Aegis brought out the platter and a bowl of chips, I took half of a roast beef sandwich and started to eat it. Sandy reluctantly accepted a sandwich, but her mind clearly was elsewhere. Still, she needed something in her stomach.

"Well, Derek's calling in everyone," Delia said, returning to the living room and sitting down. She leaned back in the chair, closing her eyes for a moment.

"Can you stay for a while?" Sandy asked.

Delia let out a long sigh. "For a few minutes." She held up her phone, reluctantly staring at the screen. "And here comes another call." She punched the button and held the phone to her ear. A few seconds later, she jumped to her feet. "Where? Keep them till we get there."

"Is it something about Jenna?" Sandy asked, her shoulders stiffening.

"Yes," Delia said, stuffing her phone back in her pocket. "Derek found Jenna and a group of kids in the graveyard, getting drunk."

"Come on," Sandy said, grabbing her coat.

"Do you want Aegis and me to come with you?" I asked.

She nodded. "Max, will you drive?"

"Text us the location," Aegis said to Delia. He turned to me. "I'll drive, you rest."

THE SEEDIER SIDE OF BEDLAM WAS ON THE NORTHWEST SIDE of the island, and it was called the Balefrost district. There wasn't a whole lot of violent crime on the island, and what there was, was met with swift and unflinching punishment, but the Balefrost district was home to some of the more questionable members of the Otherkin community.

It was where the petty thieves and other lowlifes lived. One of my friends actually lived in the Balefrost district. Garret James was a snake shifter, and he was a Dirt Witch. He was highly skilled with root work and Dirt Magic, and he was a member of the Blue Diamond Copperhead Clan in the Blue Ridge Mountains of Kentucky. He was also one of the most reliable friends I had.

As we wound through the streets, the houses became more dilapidated, the yards more overgrown. The energy was shadier and it always made me shiver as we entered the district. A number of ghosts congregated here, drawn by the chaotic magic.

We were headed toward Garret's house, and I wondered if he had had anything to do with reporting Jenna and her friends. He certainly wouldn't enable their behavior. But as we pulled up, I realized we were at the graveyard directly adjacent to his house.

From the street, his house look like a broken-down shanty, but when you got close enough to break through the glamour, it was actually a prim, well-tended cottage. Garrett kept the glamour up to ward off burglars.

As we headed toward the graveyard, I spotted a patrol car down the street. It had to be Derek's. Sandy was glowering, a scowl replacing the worry.

Delia opened the gate to the sidewalk leading through the graveyard, and we entered. I shivered. This area wasn't just haunted, it was haunted by the ghosts that didn't want to leave the physical plane. The spirits who were problem causers.

"I will beat her butt raw," Sandy muttered.

"No, you won't, and you know it." I shook my head,

giving her a faint grin. "Remember, she sees us partying hard, and she may just want to follow in your footsteps."

There was no way Sandy and I could get around it. We were party girls, and Jenna had seen us tie one on more than once. I had the feeling that it might be her way of trying to get closer to Sandy. I could be wrong, but I was also pretty astute.

"She *knows* she's not allowed to drink." Sandy stopped, freezing in her tracks. "I just realized something. The levels on several bottles in the liquor cabinet have been going down, even though I haven't been drinking from them. I asked Max but he hasn't either, so I just assumed it was my imagination. I wonder if she's been getting into the booze at home."

"Well, you can ask her." I nodded to the others, who were still walking ahead of us. "Come on, let's catch up."

Another two minutes saw us around a curve and into a widespread clearing of snow-covered grass, dotted by tombstones. There, standing with heads down, were Jenna and three of her classmates. Derek Lindsey was standing over them, scowling. I sensed some sort of magic surrounding the kids, and realized he had put up a Boundary spell, a common hex used among police officers who worked magic. It prevented people from running away. He must have used it on the kids before they managed to scatter.

Derek looked up as we approached. "I got a call about activity in the graveyard, and this is what I found."

Jenna was there, along with two boys and another girl. A few scattered bottles were on the ground next to them, and from here I could see there were two wine bottles and a vodka bottle. The wine bottles looked empty, but the vodka bottle still was about half full. The kids all looked a little loopy. They were wavering back and forth, their eyes glassy.

Sandy marched over to Jenna as Derek let down the Boundary spell. "What the hell are you doing out here? And why didn't you answer your phone? You had me worried sick!"

Jenna just stared at the ground, biting her lip. "I'm sorry, okay? I won't do it again, all right?" Although her voice was sullen, I could see the worry in her eyes that she had fucked things up for good.

"No, it's *not all right*. And I'm pretty sure you're just sorry because you got caught." Sandy turned to Delia. "What's the procedure? Are you going to run them in?"

"Well, they were drinking and they shouldn't have been. I don't see any signs of vandalism, but I don't want them running off scot-free." She glanced at the two boys and the other girl. "The three of you I've seen before. This isn't your first go-around with law enforcement, is it?"

One of the boys sullenly shook his head. "No, ma'am."

"All right, here's what we're going to do. Derek, we'll take these three back to the station and call their parents. I happen to know they're all from out of town. We'll also call the headmaster, and I'm afraid we're going to have to tell him Jenna was with them. But Jenna can go with you, Sandy. You make sure to impress on her just what a tightrope she's walking." She turned to Jenna. "Listen, little miss, you're damned lucky your mother lives here on the island. This sort of thing can get you *expelled* from Neverfall. Do you want that?"

Jenna shook her head, fighting back tears. "No. I don't want that."

"This one will be on your record. This is your first strike. Two more and you're done there. Do you understand?"

"Yeah, I get it." Jenna raised her head, tears streaking her face. "I'm sorry, okay? I'm *really* sorry."

"I'm sure the headmaster will be talking to you as well." Delia turned to Max and Sandy. "Okay, get her out of here. Derek, help me get these kids back to the cars."

"I'll see you tomorrow," I told Sandy. This was a family situation for them to work out on their own. Aegis and I returned to our car and headed home.

By the time we got home, we had thoroughly dissected the situation, along with speculating about a dozen different ways that Sandy and Max might react. As I opened the sliding glass door to the kitchen, Kelson was rinsing the dishes and putting them into the dishwasher. She looked up from the sink as we entered the room.

"Did you find Jenna?"

I nodded. "Yeah. Or rather, the police did. Drunk, in a graveyard, with a group of friends. I have a feeling somebody's going to be facing a long timeout." The air hung heavy with the scent of popcorn, and I glanced around, but didn't see anything. "The guests asked for popcorn?"

"Actually, they asked if they could help make popcorn balls. I didn't think it would hurt, so I said yes. We spent the last hour making popcorn balls and fudge. There's some on the table, if you like."

I glanced at the table, spotting the platter of fudge and popcorn balls. "By any chance is that *peppermint* fudge?"

"There might be a good chance, so why don't you try a piece and find out?" Kelson laughed, waiting for us to sit down. "Do you want some coffee to go with that? Or hot cocoa?"

"You know I never turn down coffee," I said, sliding into a chair. "But a mocha might be nice, the best of both worlds." I leaned back in my chair, biting into the fudge. It was still slightly warm, and soft enough to melt in my mouth. The warm flavors of chocolate and peppermint flooded onto my tongue. I closed my eyes, savoring the moment. "This is so good. You outdid yourself on this one."

"I have to admit, I'm not the one who made it. Henry made it. He's got talents I never dreamed he did. I just oversaw the production line. Three of the other guests—the Douglas couple and Annie Wood—made the popcorn balls. I told them I would clean up. I believe they're in the guest parlor if you'd like to say good night to them."

I let out a sigh. I didn't feel like getting up, but it would be the polite thing to do. I looked at Aegis. "We should, you know. We are the hosts."

"Come on, woman. Let's go." He held out his hand, and I took it. We strolled hand-in-hand toward the room that used to be the grand ballroom, and he slid his arm around my waist. "How are you feeling tonight?"

"Still bruised, like an overripe peach. I wish my rib would just hurry up and heal. But Jordan tells me it's going to be another two or three weeks till I can breathe normally. Craig sure did a number on me."

"In some ways, I wish he had lived, because if I had gotten to him before Franny did, I would have torn him limb from limb." Aegis lowered, shaking his head. "I will always feel like I failed in protecting you."

"Stop that," I said as we approached the double doors leading into the guest parlor. "We can only do what we can. Trust me, he was afraid before he died. You should have seen his face when he saw Franny."

Aegis opened the doors, escorting me in. All of our guests were in the parlor, gathered around the piano. Nancy Douglas was playing carols, and they were all singing together. It was a picture-perfect moment, so I flipped out my phone.

"Don't stop! Do you mind if I take a picture for our website?"

No one objected, so I took several pictures of them gathered around the piano with fudge, mugs of hot cocoa, and popcorn balls, with the tree in back of them. It would be perfect for advertising.

"We wanted to come wish you a good evening, and a restful night," Aegis said.

The Douglases were human, and they still weren't sure what to make of Aegis being a vampire. But the way Nancy Douglas looked at him told me that his glamour went a long way in making them friendly.

"Thank you," Henry said, finishing off his cocoa. "If everybody's done, I'll just carry this tray of dishes back into the kitchen. I don't want Kelson to have to go to any trouble for us."

"You don't have to do that," I said. "It's her job, and ours, to make your stay here comfortable."

He let out a laugh, his glasses sliding down his nose. Pushing them back up, he said, "This is my home away from home. I don't mind helping out." He stacked the mugs and dessert plates on a tray, and carried them out of the room.

"I hope you're all enjoying your stay here," I said to the other guests.

There was a murmur of assent, and Carol Radcliffe, Annie Wood's roommate, said, "Bedlam is one of the most beautiful places I've ever seen. I've heard a lot about it from my cousin, who is a rat-shifter. Her father is my uncle. He married a rat-shifter and Lori inherited her mother's abilities."

"Do they live here on the island?" I asked.

Carol shook her head. "No, but they've come here before to visit. Apparently, my aunt has relatives who live here." She paused, then asked, "Do you mind if I ask you a question?"

"Go right ahead."

"I'm not sure how it all works. If a shifter marries a human, wouldn't the children be half shifter, half human?"

I bit my lip for a moment, trying to think about what I knew about shifter heritages. "I don't think so. I believe that the children of a mixed marriage involving shifters either inherit their mother's heritage or their father's. I think it's sort of all or nothing."

"That would make sense," Carol said. "My cousin has two brothers who have no abilities whatsoever in terms of shifting form."

"It's snowing up a gale outside," Aegis said, peeking out the window. "I'm afraid we might be snowed in during the morning, so I'll go out early and dig out the cars as best as I can. But I urge you to take caution on the roads."

With that, we made our good nights and headed back to our own parlor. It was cozier than the living room, and we spent a lot of time there. Aegis stoked the fire as I settled into a rocking chair and put my feet up on an ottoman. I shivered and spread a throw over my legs. The Bewitching Bedlam was a drafty old mansion, even though we had plugged up as many of the holes as we could find. But all houses this size were large and chilly during the winter, no matter how well-built they were. I loved the place, though. In a little over a year it had become my home and my haven.

"Are you tired?" Aegis asked. "I thought you might help me with a jigsaw puzzle before I start my baking."

"Actually, I'm exhausted. I thought I might go up to bed early, if you don't mind." I hated taking time away from us, but our schedules were on opposite cycles, and it was just a fact we had to adapt to.

"I'll come up and say good night to you, then. What would you like me to bake tonight?" Aegis swept me up in his arms and I draped one arm around his shoulders. I had long ago given up objecting to him carrying me up to bed. He liked it, and it was a comfortable routine.

"Gingerbread cookies, peppermint brownies, and a couple of spiced peach pies."

"I think I'll also make scones and teacakes. It's bread-making time again too, so I'm going to whip up a couple loaves of sourdough."

"Say, weren't you guys supposed to rehearse tonight?"

"Yeah, but Sid called while we was over at Sandy and Max's. His wife is sick, so we're calling off rehearsal for this week. We don't have a gig until January, so we're good for now." He sounded worried.

"Sick? What do you mean sick? Like the flu or cold?"

He shook his head. "I think it's worse than that. Sid

didn't say very much, but I could hear the concern in his voice. He was far more abrupt than usual."

Sid was a bassist with the Boys of Bedlam, Aegis's Celtic rock band. He and his wife, Sylvia, were Fae. They had five children: two sets of twins and a baby who still wasn't into the toddler stage yet.

"You should go visit and see how she is."

Aegis shook his head. "Not until Sid is ready to open up. As I said, I get the feeling this is something major. He'll talk when he's ready, and until then I don't want to push him. Meanwhile, Jorge is spending the holidays with his family in Seattle, and Keth and his girlfriend went on a ski trip to Crystal Mountain."

The thought of a half satyr on skis made me giggle.

We reached the top of the stairs, and Aegis let me down. I opened the door to my bedroom, and he followed me in. Bubba and Luna came racing in behind us. They bounced on the bed, Luna rolling over on her back for belly rubs. Bubba just sat. He knew better than that.

Aegis sat down as I stripped off my clothes and tossed them in the laundry basket. The bruises on my hip were starting to fade. They had passed the black and blue stage, and were now a nauseating yellow and purple. Aegis unhooked my bra, since I couldn't reach it without pain, and handed me the lingerie bra I wore at night.

"I am so ready to drop." I crawled into bed.

"Then sleep well, my love." Aegis leaned over, planting his lips on mine. He gave me a long, slow kiss, but it was delicate and gentle. He tucked me into bed, and as he turned to leave, Bubba and Luna curled up on my feet.

"Good night," I said.

"Sleep until morning," he whispered, leaving the door ajar just enough so that the cats could get out.

Barely five minutes passed before I started to drift off. Luna lay down, pressing her body against my back. Her body warmth comforted me as Bubba warmed my feet, and I finally drifted off, falling into a dreamless slumber until morning.

CHAPTER NINE

I slept late the next morning, and when I woke up, I realized that my alarm hadn't gone off. Groggy, I eased myself into a sitting position and glanced at the clock. It was almost nine. Outside, I saw that it was still snowing, big thick flakes coming down to shroud the island. I shivered as I threw back the covers, the chill of the morning hitting me. I glanced at my nightstand and there was a note from Aegis, along with a delicious-looking brownie.

> My sweet, I hope you slept well. Everything went smoothly during the night, and all the baked goods are on the counter, waiting for Kelson. I shoveled out all the cars, and since we were running low on groceries, I made a quick trip to the Shop Mart and stocked up on eggs, milk, sausage, and a few other things to tide us over. I also turned off your alarm so

you could get some more sleep. I'll see you tonight, and take care of yourself. Love, -A-

---

I smiled as I set the note aside.

Every night, Aegis left me a note on my nightstand and I kept them all, tucking them into a velvet box. I bit into the brownie, sighing happily as the tastes of peppermint and chocolate filled my senses. It might not be a proper breakfast, but it sure helped wake me up.

After eating some more of the brownie, I took a shower and then dried my hair. I chose a wraparound skirt and a V-neck sweater that was easy enough to put on. My bra was problematic, but I could fasten it in front and then gently slide it around and ease my arms through the straps. It took me twice as long as normal, but it worked.

I fastened a corset belt around my waist, strapping it snugly but not too tight. It helped ease the ache in my rib cage. Finally, I slipped on a pair of ballet flats and, after fixing my makeup, I finished off the last of the brownie and headed downstairs.

Kelson was in the kitchen. She glanced up as I came in and she pointed to the table. "Breakfast is on. Sit down and eat up, and I'll get your mocha."

Breakfast consisted of toast and sausage, and a couple hard-boiled eggs. Kelson handed me my mocha and I thanked her, carrying it to the office with me. As I unlocked the door and clipped my keys to my belt, a voice tinkled out from the room.

"I'm here," Franny said. "I didn't want to startle you."

"Thank you, especially considering I'm carrying a cup

of hot mocha." I shut the door behind me and turned to see her sitting in the side chair next to my desk. "And how are you on this snowy morning?"

She laughed again. "It's so beautiful. And it's so nice to get out of the house and be able to walk in the snow. I don't mind admitting that it's nice to not feel the chill while I'm out there. One of the few benefits of being dead, I guess."

"So what are you up to?" I asked as I sat down at my desk and carefully placed my mocha on a coaster.

"I've been talking to Franz, that stray ghost who is out in the yard. We're working on trying to pinpoint how he died." She leaned one elbow on my desk, and the tip of it sank through the surface.

"So you know his name?"

She shook her head. "No, I just think he looks like a Franz. We've been going all over the island, trying to find places that look familiar to him."

"Why don't you talk to Delia? She can have you look through the missing-persons photos. Maybe you'll recognize him."

Franny clapped her hands. "That's a wonderful idea. I really do want to help him. He seems so incredibly sad. I may have been bound in this house for a couple hundred years, but at least I knew who I was, and how I died." She sobered, and I realized this meant a lot to her.

"I'll call her in a few minutes and make arrangements for you to go down to the police station."

"Thank you. Just call for me when she's ready. I'll stick close by." And with that, she vanished.

After listening to the messages, and putting three more people on the bed-and-breakfast waitlist, I was about to give Delia a call when my phone rang. Speak of the devil.

"Hey, I was about to call you," I said. "Franny would like to look over your file of missing persons. She's met a ghost and he can't remember who he is. She's taking it up on herself to help him figure it out. We thought that maybe he was someone who'd gone missing on the island, so if you're up to having her come down there, I'll send her right away."

"That's fine. Send her down. She'll have to manifest to talk to one of my officers, but there's no problem having her in the building."

"Fine, I don't think she'll object. So, you were calling me?"

Delia let out a long sigh, and I knew something else had gone wrong. "I have a serious problem and I need you down here. You and Sandy, if you would bring her. There's some sort of demon hanging out in the town square, and he's being incredibly annoying."

"Say what? A *demon* in the town square? What the hell is he doing, throwing people around?"

"No, he's not throwing people around. It's worse. He's…peeing in the fountain. And making lewd gestures at passing women. If I didn't know better, I'd swear he was drunk."

I stared at my phone for a moment. "Maybe we should look at getting rid of the fountain. It's attracting some weird-ass energy lately."

"Very funny. So will you and Sandy come down?" Delia sounded put out.

"Yes," I hastily said. "I'll come down. Meanwhile, don't antagonize him."

"I have no idea what to do with him. I could try to throw him in jail, but he's a demon. While our cells are magic-proof, I don't know if they can hold a demon."

"How do you *know* he's a demon?"

"Well, he looks like one. I could be wrong, but usually, what you see is what you get."

"All right, I'll call Sandy, and then I'll head out. It might take me half an hour, given the state of the roads, but I'll be there. And I'll send Franny down to the station and remind her to make herself visible. Will you tell someone she's on her way? It will only take her a few seconds."

"Tell her to give me five minutes. And I'll meet you by the fountain as soon as you can make it." Without another word, she hung up.

As I pocketed my phone, I called out, "Franny? Franny!"

"You rang?" She popped into the room.

"Give Delia five minutes, then show up at the police station. You'll need to make yourself visible and tell them why you're there, but she'll have someone waiting for you. Good luck!"

"Thanks ever so much." Once again, she clapped her hands, and then she vanished.

I locked the office, chugging the rest of my mocha as I headed back toward the kitchen. "Hey, Kelson, I need to go downtown. Delia needs me. Hold down the fort here, okay?"

"It's a good thing Aegis put snow tires on the Lexus. I'd feel better if you were driving the CRV, but beggars can't be choosers."

"I'd feel better if I were driving my SUV too, but as you said… All right, if you'd help me on with my boots, because bending over is still a pain in the side, I'd appreciate it." As long as I had someone there to help, there was no sense in making myself ache any more than I had to. As soon as I had my boots on, I bundled into my coat and called Sandy. I filled her in on what was going on, and asked her to meet me downtown.

"I'll be there. I'll leave Jenna with Alex. She knows better than screw up again so soon. She's been suspended from Neverfall for the rest of the semester. That's not saying much, given the winter holidays are coming up, but it still made an impression on her. At least I hope it did."

"I'll see you down there, and drive safe. The roads are treacherous."

And with that, I headed out the door, into the still-falling snow that had muffled the world into silence. I just hoped that the peaceful morning wouldn't be too marred by the demon. And that, whoever he was, Sandy and I would be able to handle him without too much of a problem.

I WAS SITTING IN THE CAR, WAITING FOR IT TO WARM UP, when my phone rang. I glanced at it. I didn't recognize the number. "Hello?" I said, wishing the snow on my windshield would melt faster.

"Maddy?" The voice sounded familiar.

"Yes, who—" But I was cut off as the voice continued.

"I love you, Maddy. I miss you and I can't stop thinking about you. We'll be together soon, and nothing will ever separate us again." The phone went silent as the call ended.

I stared at the screen. "*Crap*." I tried calling the number back, but nobody answered. Nervous, and starting to feel spooked, I decided to ask Delia to look up the number for me and see where it was coming from.

I put the car in gear and headed toward town, managing to navigate around several spinouts and accidents. As I eased into a parking spot near the fountain and cautiously stepped out onto the snow-covered sidewalks, the flurry of snow grew thicker. It was coming down hard in huge wet flakes. I pulled on a ski cap that Auntie Tautau had knitted for me. It was a beautiful purple, with silver threads running through it. That reminded me to call Auntie Tautau again and leave another message, for whatever good it would do.

It didn't take me long to find Delia. All I had to do was follow the shouts. As I was headed over, I saw Sandy getting out of her car. She slammed the door, then dashed over toward me. How she managed to keep upright on the slick surface, I didn't know, but Sandy was athletic and managed things like that better than I did.

"What's going on?" Sandy asked.

"I'm not sure. Something about a demon." I glanced at the car. "Did you leave Jenna at home?"

She nodded. "Yeah, and boy did we have words last night. I'll tell you about it later. Neither one of us are happy campers at this point."

We rounded the fountain to see Delia standing there, hands on her hips as she stared at a very large, very brutish-looking demon. He was a good eight feet high, and he was half goat, half something else. His upper torso was shaped like a man, only he was covered in fur. A yellowish white, the hair was streaked with gray and black and it trailed down like scarves.

His face was horrific, with two curving horns that arched back over his head. His eyes were stark white, with black irises, and his pupils were glowing red. His nose was bulbous, and when he opened his mouth, sharp fangs replaced the canids, much like a vampire's, only thick and yellowed. His other teeth reminded me of normal human teeth, and his gums were red, as though covered with blood. His ears stood out to the side, reminding me of a bat's wings.

The bottom of his torso, from his waist down, was also heavily furred, just like a satyr. His legs were thick and muscled, ending in cloven hooves, also like a satyr. It was obvious he was male, and frankly, the size of his cock terrified me. No satyr had *ever* been that well endowed.

"Oh my God, look at that—" Sandy started to say.

"I know, I can't take my eyes off of it," I sputtered.

Delia gave us an annoyed look. "Once you guys are finished assessing his attributes, can you *do* something? I don't even know how to talk to him."

"Why do you think *we* can talk to demons?" I asked.

"I don't know, but you *are* the High Priestess of the Moonrise Coven, so it's up to you to help me out in situations like this. It's in the town covenant." Technically, she was right. That didn't mean I could do anything.

I pulled my gaze away from his nether regions and stepped forward. Clearing my throat, I decided to start with the obvious. "Hi. Who are you?"

He had been sitting on the edge of the fountain, trying to break off pieces of the rock. At least, it looked like that was what he was doing. Now, at the sound of my voice, he looked up, his eyes narrowing.

"Thrakarat!"

"I'm sorry, I don't speak whatever language that is. Do you know English?" At least I had his attention, which wasn't exactly comforting.

He paused for a moment, staring at me with those chilling eyes. Finally, in a guttural voice, he said, "Who are you?"

I let out a sigh. So far, this wasn't going very well. But at least he could speak English, unless he was just mimicking my words. "My name is Maddy. What's your name?"

Another pause, and then, still in a voice that was so low it almost shook the street, he said, "Krampus. Where am I?"

Uh-oh. If he really *was* Krampus, we had trouble on our hands. Then, the second part of his answer hit me. I glanced back at Delia. "I wonder if he really doesn't know where he's at. If so, this reminds me of the gnomes."

"Gnomes? I hate gnomes! If I see any gnomes I will squash them flat," Krampus said.

I sighed. This was *so not* how I intended to spend the morning. I quickly searched for something to say. "Do you really not know where you are? How did you get here?"

"I don't know where I am and I have no idea how I got here. I was at home, getting ready for the morning hunt, when all of a sudden, here I am. Apparently in the middle of hell." He looked around, shaking his head. "Too much noise, too much light, and too much joy."

I took a step back, motioning for Delia and Sandy to come closer.

"I really think he *is* Krampus. According to all reports I've read, Krampus has a real problem with joy, and he doesn't live in the city. The question is, how the hell did he get here? Maybe the same way the gnomes did? Do you think there's a rogue portal in our town that we don't know about?"

"I doubt if the gnomes come from the same place Krampus does," Sandy said.

"Maybe not, but I don't have anything else to go on. What the hell do we do with him? How do we get rid of him? We can't put him on a plane and send him back to wherever he came from." I paused, then asked, "Where *does* he come from?"

"Europe. Somewhere in central Europe," Delia said, horrified. "I can't let him run around the island. Can we just ask him to leave?"

I turned back to Krampus, edging forward. "Excuse me, Krampus. Is it possible that you can just go home on your own?"

He spat, the trail of spittle landing at my feet. I jumped back a step.

"If I could go home, don't you think I would have already gone? Now tell me, where am I?"

I really didn't want to give them the name of the town, because I didn't want him to remember it. "Have you heard of the United States of America?"

He gave me a look that bordered between disgusted and perplexed. "Yes. I have."

"You're there. You're on an island in the United States of America. We would love nothing more than to send you home, but we have to figure out how. Will you excuse me a moment?"

He grunted, and I took that as a yes. I hightailed it back to Delia and Sandy, motioning for them to follow me a little ways to the side.

"He says he would go home if he could figure out how. I haven't told him the name of the island or the town yet. Somehow, I don't think that would be a good idea. I can just imagine him trying to get revenge. So, what do we do?"

At that moment, we heard someone coming toward us.

"Well, if it isn't my two young friends."

"Auntie Tautau?" I asked, swinging around. "Thank gods you're here."

She laughed and looked at Krampus. "I see you have an unwelcome visitor. I thought I might be of some use."

Krampus jumped up. "One of the Aunties. I didn't do it! I wasn't the one who came here! Don't punish me, please."

Watching the demon begging the little old lady who was wearing a floral housedress under a bulky parka not to hurt him was more than I could take. I started to laugh, which only made me hurt, but I couldn't stop.

Auntie Tautau glanced over at me. "It's no laughing matter, girl. The web around the island is severely out of whack. And it's only going to get worse unless we fix it."

CHAPTER TEN

Auntie Tautau shook her head, pushing through us to address Krampus. "There, there," she said. "We know you didn't come here voluntarily. Can you tell me what happened right before you showed up here?"

Krampus gave her a hangdog look. "I was just checking my schedule for the day, and making preparations for the upcoming parade, when everything around me seemed to waver and I heard some sort of staticky sound. The next moment, I was here, sitting by the fountain."

Auntie Tautau turned to Delia, Sandy, and me. "I *told* you that there's something off with Bedlam's aura. And I've figured out what it is. The Touchstone is out of alignment. That earthquake we had a few weeks ago—the one over on the mainland—shook it off-kilter."

I stared at her for a moment. "*Touchstone?*" This was the first time I'd heard of Bedlam having a touchstone. I didn't even know what a touchstone *was*.

Auntie Tautau smiled. "That's right, I don't believe I've

told you and Sandy about it. I assumed you knew, but… Delia knows about it." She glanced at Krampus. "Krampus, would you mind if we whisk you away from the town square? We'll be able to send you home, but not at this very moment. It won't take long, I promise, so if you would cooperate with us we'll escort you to one of our guest quarters."

Delia started to say something, but Auntie Tautau held up her hand.

Krampus let out a huge sigh. He looked deflated, and he gave us a little shrug. "I'm not an unreasonable man. All right. If you can get me home by tomorrow, I'll cooperate."

"You have my word," Auntie Tautau said. I wasn't sure if she was lying or not, but it worked. Auntie Tautau turned to Delia. "Why don't you take Krampus back to the guest hotel, and make sure he's settled in one of *your rooms?*"

Delia stared at her, uncomprehending, but I suddenly caught on to what she meant. I yanked Delia to the side.

"She's talking about the jail," I whispered into her ear.

Delia's eyes widened. She turned back to Krampus. "Of course. I don't mind at all. Please come with me? I'm afraid you'll have to walk behind my car because I don't think you'll fit."

Krampus shrugged. "I don't like vehicles anyway. I won't cause any more trouble. So, do you serve lunch in your…hotel?"

I had a feeling that Krampus was onto what we were talking about, but at least he was being reasonable and not making a scene. Delia led him away. He followed her squad car as she slowly began to drive toward City Hall.

Once they were out of earshot, I turned back to Auntie Tautau. "Just what is this Touchstone?"

"Can we go somewhere warm?" Auntie Tautau asked. "Perhaps the diner over there?" She nodded to one of the local diners.

Sandy and I followed her through the doors. We settled into the booth, and after we ordered hot chocolate and peach cobbler, Auntie Tautau began to explain.

"Every magical town has a Touchstone, a gem that embodies the energy of the town. The founders of Bedlam were no exception. The Touchstone is secreted in Enchanted Sands Park. It's a large sapphire, and you'll find it at the base of Arianrhod's statue. I thought that Linda would have shown you, but then again, she didn't have much time when you took her place as High Priestess. I never even thought about it until the aura got dislodged. The Touchstone keeps the magical energy surrounding Bedlam in order and keeps it from becoming too chaotic."

"So what do I have to do?"

"Go to the park after sunset and opened the secret panel. The stone has to be out of alignment. You will see where it's *supposed* to be—there's an indentation that holds it in place in the compartment under the statue. It probably got jolted to the side. Once you set it back into place, Bedlam's aura will realign itself, and we won't have random chaos like strangers showing up from storybooks or demons milling around town. At least not randomly. We're lucky we didn't attract somebody far worse than Krampus but we're not in the clear yet, so you need to do this soon."

"So all I have to do is go there tonight and take care of

this? And that will stop all the random arguing and manifestations?" It sounded almost too easy.

"Well, once you reset it, it will take a few hours, but yes —the energy surrounding the island will return to normal. No one can do so but the High Priestess, by the way. If anybody else tries to touch the gem it will disintegrate them. The defense mechanism was built into the gem at the beginning. For a long time, the High Priestess of the island took care of things, but when the official coven was formed, the power transferred to the High Priestess of the coven."

"I'm guessing that Sandy can't do it for me?"

Sandy snorted. "Sandy doesn't *want* to do it for you. Especially if the result is me turning into a crispy critter."

"No, she can't. And you should go alone. I know it's asking a lot given your current condition, but you have to take care of this *now* before something far worse happens. If the aura of the island stays out of alignment for too long, it can destabilize the entire area, and in more than just a magical sense. It could cause major earthquakes, it could set off the volcanoes...things like that." Auntie Tautau spoke as though she were discussing a recipe, or a TV show.

I coughed. "I supposed I'd better get a move on, then. I'll go tonight. It has to be done at night, correct?"

"Yes, for several reasons. One, the hustle and bustle of the day can interfere with the energy as it resets. Also, you don't want anybody there who might take it into his head to mess with the gem and disintegrate himself."

"No, we wouldn't want that," I said, laughing. I winced as I held my side. "Oh, don't get me started. Laughing still hurts." I picked up my hot cocoa and took a long sip, leaning back against the booth. At least we had an answer to what was going on lately. That was more than I could say for a lot of things.

AFTER AUNTIE TAUTAU LEFT THE DINER, SANDY AND I SAT there for a few more minutes.

Sandy told me that Jenna had abruptly come to her senses when she realized how close she was to getting kicked out of Neverfall, but there were still a number of issues to tackle.

"I've realized that I need to set a better role model for her," Sandy said. "It means backing off the partying. We can still have fun, but Maddy, I need to ease up on the booze. I never thought I'd say that, especially after all these years, but I believe in teaching by example. And I'm Jenna's mom now."

I took her hands in mine. "I understand. Believe me, I do. Don't worry about it. We can have just as much fun without getting wasted. I suppose there comes a time in all of our lives when we have to let go of old patterns and behaviors." I paused, then said, "I got a phone call this morning." I told her about the recording, and how much it had unnerved me. "I don't know who's doing this, and I'm scared."

"This is getting serious, Maddy. Have you told Delia yet?"

I shook my head. "I don't want to bother her until I've reset the Touchstone and things get back to normal. She's been so swamped lately and I really don't want to add to her worries. I'll be all right." I glanced at the clock. It was nearly noon. "Did you want to order lunch before we leave, or do you have to go right now?"

Sandy shrugged. "I'd better go. I just found out that Max's parents are coming in early. Which means I need to confront their dislike of me before our wedding and before the holidays. I really don't want to see them, Maddy. I've decided I'm going to talk to Max tonight, since they won't be in until afternoon tomorrow."

I squeezed her hands, then slid out of the booth. "If it isn't one thing, it's another. We'll get through this, and we'll get married, and settle into our lives here in Bedlam in a way that, frankly, I never expected to."

She kissed me on the cheek, then waved good-bye she headed out of the diner doors. I paid for our cobbler and hot chocolate, and—ordering a milkshake to go— cautiously headed back to my car. I had a lot to think about, and even more to do.

Aegis didn't want to let me go alone to Enchanted Sands Park, but I bluntly told him that this was just one of my tasks as High Priestess. I decided to put off telling him about the phone call until after I had reset the Touchstone. Once he found out about *that*, he wouldn't let me out of his sight and I knew it. And quite frankly, even though I would've liked to have him there, this was my job to deal with.

"Are you sure you can drive?" he asked. "I know the snow has stopped, but it's slippery and treacherous."

"I drove downtown this morning to deal with Krampus. And if I don't take care of this tonight, a lot worse could happen to the island than getting a visit from Mr. Anti-Christmas himself. At least he doesn't bother with Winter Solstice, although I have a feeling he may have in the past."

I bundled up and glanced over at Kelson. "Which reminds me, we need to order the prime rib for solstice dinner. Can you put that on the list? I'm not sure how many guests we'll have, so check the schedule. We'll also have Sandy, Max, and Jenna here, and plan for at least three more just in case we have unexpected company."

"Will do," she said.

"All right, I'm headed out now. I should be home soon. From what Auntie Tautau told me, this shouldn't take me too long. Thank gods, it's something as simple as this, although I would never have known if she hadn't mentioned it."

As I headed out to my car, Aegis stood by the door. I knew he wanted to go, but I didn't want him in any danger, and I had no idea if the stone reacted to anybody else being nearby.

I eased out of the driveway, onto the main road. The drive to Enchanted Sands Park would be dicey, but with snow tires on the Lexus I should be able to make it.

Overhead, the clouds were socking in for another go-around. I glanced out the window, staring at the soft flakes that had begun to flutter down. My mind reeling with thoughts of the wedding, thoughts of the Touch-stone, and the nagging thoughts about whoever was sending me the notes and had left me voice mail all whirled together into a loud racket that filled my head. Finally, I switched on the radio to drown them out.

CHAPTER ELEVEN

*E*nchanted Sands Park was mostly a day park, though it had a few campsites. On occasion, school groups or fraternities like the Rooks would book the sites and spend a couple days on a retreat. The park was on the edge of the island, and a rocky shore led out to the water. In the center of the park was a clearing, and in that clearing was a large statue of Arianrhod, the patron goddess of the entire town. She was also my goddess as well.

I parked in the stall closest to the statue. There was no one else around, which didn't surprise me at all. The statue was only a few minutes' walk away, but plodding through the thick snow would take some effort, especially given my hip. I had brought a walking stick with me and I had also brought my bag of magical supplies, including my wand and a dagger, and a few other assorted items that I never went on a magical mission without.

"This would be a whole lot more fun if I could have asked Sandy come with me," I muttered as I got out of the car. I made sure my jacket was zipped tight and pulled the hood over my head.

The bag of supplies was heavy enough to make my side ache, but I braced myself against my walking stick and started toward the statue. There were some days when being the High Priestess of the coven felt like it was just a lot of added responsibility. I truly didn't mind it most of the time, but right now I wanted to be inside, warm and cozy, cuddled under a blanket. The cold seeped into my bones, making me hurt even worse, and my hip wasn't happy either.

I slogged through the snow, finally making it to the base of the statue. Luckily, the panel that I was looking for wasn't buried—yet. It was at the top of the plinth—near the base of Arianrhod's feet.

Auntie Tautau had explained to me how to open it. Arianrhod's name was in a raised relief across the front of the plinth that the statue stood on. I reached out, pressing first the A, then the H, and then the D. Then I pressed the A once more.

The front of the panel with her name on it slowly opened, sliding down into the base, exposing an inner chamber about the size of a small home safe.

I set up a flashlight, propping it so that remained aimed into the chamber. As I knelt in the snow, a faint glow emanated from inside. Pale blue and sparkling, it was icy enough to match the weather. The glow shimmered out from a large sapphire the size of a peach, sitting the center of the chamber. Or at least, it *should* have been in the center. Held aloft by a platinum setting that kept it upright and in place, the sapphire shimmered with a ray of light that shot out from the faceted top. But instead of the light feeding into a circular hole directly below the center of the statue, the ray was ricocheting off the chamber walls. The gem was off-center, all right, and from here, I could feel the erratic nature of the energy. No wonder the magic surrounding Bedlam had been askew.

I caught my breath, wincing, and gingerly reached inside. I hoped to hell that Auntie Tautau was right and that the stone would recognize me as the High Priestess of the coven. Otherwise, this was going to be one hell of a short adventure, and the last in my life.

The sapphire crackled, its magic wrapping around my hand as my fingers drew near. I paused, holding my breath, as it probed my energy field. I closed my eyes, just in case it might get the wrong idea, but a moment later nothing had happened and I opened my eyes again. Apparently, the gem had accepted my credentials.

I slowly let out my breath, then began to move the jewel back beneath the hole. There were markers on the base of the plinth indicating where the stand should rest, and I eased the sapphire back in place. As I settled it on to the marks, I heard a *click*, and the light began to stream up through the statue. I had often wondered what made Arianrhod's statue glow, and now I knew. I leaned back, thinking it couldn't be that easy, but that's what Auntie Tautau had told me to do.

"I should superglue this down," I said as I closed the panel and pushed myself to my feet. "At least that's done and things should get back to normal."

As I turned, I heard a noise. A dark figure was standing near me.

"Hello?" I asked warily.

The figure said nothing. From where I was standing I

could tell I was facing a man, but I couldn't see his features. I began to get nervous. Why hadn't I let Aegis come? He could have stayed in the car, but no, I had to be too stubborn.

"Who are you? What do you want?"

Before I could even blink, the figure moved in a blur and was standing in front of me. He leaned down. In the faint glow of the snow and the light from the statue, I suddenly recognized his face.

"Maddy, I've missed you so much. I've come for you." Before I could move away, Tom reached out and grabbed my wrist, pulling me to him.

My sweet Tom was back, and I was scared out of my wits.

"Oh my gods, Tom! What are you doing here?"

It *couldn't* be him. Not only had he been captured by vampires, but he had been turned, and then thrown into some horrid dimension with a violent monster watching him. The last time I saw him, he had managed to come to his senses long enough to tell me to run. I had managed to get away before he could latch onto me, and I had left him in my past.

He *couldn't* be here, in Bedlam, standing right in front of me.

"It can't be you," I said, trying to pull away. But he held me fast, and an inner alarm rang loud and clear. I was in danger.

"I missed you so much. Since I last saw you, all I could think of was getting free and finding you again.

And now I've finally done it. I know you still love me, even though I'm a vampire. You loved me before, and now you're with a vampire, so you can't hate me like you once hated all of my kind. Come back to me, Maddy. Come with me." He was pleading, his eyes fully crimson. His hand held my wrist so tightly that it felt like he might break my bones.

"You have to let me go. You don't belong here. Please, leave me alone."

But the look in his eyes told me he was no longer rational. My sweet Tom had truly turned into *Mad Tom*. My heart raced as memories flooded my mind—memories of his touch, his smile. Memories of the love we had shared. But I had walked away from them when I met Aegis. I had left those memories behind and embraced my present.

"Tom, I loved you more than I loved life itself. But that's in the past. So much as happened since then. I'm not your Mad Maudlin, and you're not my sweet Tom anymore."

A snarl crossed his face, and he pulled me to him, wrapping his arm roughly around my waist. I screamed, the pain from my fractured rib ricocheting through me.

"You always were *mine*, and you'll always be mine. I tried to let you go, but I couldn't. The thought of you turning your back on me is more than I can bear. At first I stayed away because I was a vampire and I knew how much you hated what I had become. But now things are different. You claim to love a vampire. You fuck him. You've betrayed who you were, but in doing so you've paved the way for me to return to your life." He kissed me, savagely forcing his tongue between my lips. I tried to brace my hands against his shoulders, to push him away, but he was far too strong.

He slid one hand under my shirt, reaching up to squeeze my breast so hard that it hurt. I let out a yelp and struggled, managing to break free from the kiss.

"I beg you. If you *ever* loved me, then let me go. Tom, don't do something that will make me hate you forever." I was crying now. I knew that if I didn't get free, he would take me with him and life would never be the same. He'd turn me, and I'd end up hating him forever.

"Oh no, my girl," he said, sounding like he was enjoying the struggle. "My sweet, you're going with me. We'll be together like we always planned. You ran wild after I was turned. You terrorized my kind, destroying everything that reminded you of what they did to me. But I'm *part* of their world, and you will be, too. You'll never leave my side again." He reared, his fangs extending as he aimed for my throat.

I screamed one last, loud scream.

As he descended, I braced myself for the impact, but the next thing I knew the impact actually came from the side. Something sent me flying against the nearest snowbank.

Groaning, I sat up just in time to see Aegis wrestling with Tom. They were rolling in the snow, vampire against vampire. Aegis was stronger than Tom, but Tom was truly mad and madness brought its own strength.

I forced myself to my feet and fumbled in my bag. I had my stake with me, the one I had used in my journeys across Europe. I pulled it out and stared at the silver blade. More than just a dagger, it had been specifically fashioned for me so I could hunt down vampires. I had sworn never to use it again, but when Essie—Queen of the Pacific Northwest Vampire Nation—had crossed my path, I had brought it out again, just in case.

I turned toward the brawling vampires, my heart aching as my old love fought my new one. I couldn't let Tom hurt Aegis. I couldn't let him destroy the man I loved. I stumbled forward as they churned through the snow, snarling and growling, slicing at each other with their nails, fangs bared, trying to gain the advantage. I knew what I had to do.

"Tom, leave Aegis alone. I'll go with you." I held the stake behind me as I extended my other hand to him. "Please, let Aegis live and I will go with you. I give you my word." Even as I made an oath I knew I was destined to break, the words hurt my heart.

Tom threw Aegis across the snow and turned to me. "You mean it?" In his frenzy, he heard my words, not the emotions behind them.

I nodded. "Come closer. I want to give you a kiss."

"Maddy!" Aegis called out, raw pain filling his voice. "Don't, please don't!"

I kept my eyes on Tom as the vampire drew near. He still looked like my love, still sounded like him, but the Tom I had known and loved was gone forever. He hadn't been able to keep hold of his humanity like Aegis had managed to. The vampires had tortured Tom before they turned him, and there was no way back from the abyss.

"Come closer. I want to be with you," I said, choking on my words.

His expression almost that of a child's, Tom hurried toward me, his eyes glowing. "I knew you'd pick me. I knew that you still loved me."

He was close enough to touch and I held out my hand for his. He took it, and I gave him one last smile. "Oh Tom, you don't know how hard this is for me. I loved you, please remember that. I loved you to the ends of the earth and back."

Before he could speak I thrust the spike forward, my rib cage screaming with the movement. The sharp tip plunged into Tom's chest and I threw myself forward, knocking him to the ground as I drove the stake through his heart. The oddest look of surprise and dismay filled his eyes, and then, before he could say more than "Maddy," he vanished in a flurry of dust.

My sweet Tom was gone forever.

CHAPTER TWELVE

*E*verything was a blur after that, Aegis bundled me up, carrying me back to the car. Instead of going home, he drove directly to Jordan Farrows's place. Jordan was my doctor, and he opened the door when Aegis banged his fist against it.

"Maddy's hurt," Aegis said, pushing past him into the house. "Please, help her?"

Jordan didn't even register surprise. He was used to people bursting in on him in the middle of the night. He motioned for Aegis to carry me into a back room. While he had an office at the medical center, Jordan also kept a home office for unusual cases and middle of the night emergencies. Aegis placed me on the exam table, hovering over me.

"What happened?" Jordan asked.

"A vampire tried to attack her. I'm not sure if he managed to bite her or not, but I know she's injured." He brushed the hair out of my face, leaning down to kiss my forehead. "I can't believe that you put your life on the line for me. Maddy, don't *ever* do that again. I thought I was going to lose you."

Through the haze of pain that radiated through my ribs and torso, I could hear the fear in Aegis's voice.

"Move," Jordan instructed him, motioning for him to move aside. "We'll need to take off her shirt and jacket. I doubt she can raise her arms. I'd like to cut them off, if you don't mind."

I started to protest but all that came out was a gasp of pain. Jordan ignored it, reaching for the scissors. Together, he and Aegis cut the shirt and jacket off my body. I could barely breathe, and Jordan very gently examined my ribs, then looked up at Aegis.

"I have a feeling that she's cracked another one or two. And her hand looks injured. We need to get her to the hospital."

"In that storm out there, I don't know if an ambulance can make it here."

"We can take her in the car, if you can drive. I can't take the x-rays here that I need to assess her condition."

Thirty painful minutes later, I was on an exam table at the hospital, with the tech taking pictures of my torso. It was all I could do to grunt when he moved me, even though the pain was bad enough to make me want to scream. I couldn't take a deep-enough breath for that. Another hour and I was in a bed in the hospital, leaning back against the raised mattress. Jordan and Aegis were standing beside me, and I was pleasantly numb thanks to the pain medication that Jordan had prescribed. It was one that was safe for witches to take.

"Well, this time you have *three* more cracked ribs. And you also have a fractured wrist. I'm not letting you go home tonight. The roads are too dangerous for that. And I want to keep an eye on those ribs to make sure they don't move. So consider yourself effectively immobilized. Welcome to the hospital." Jordan grinned at me. He turned Aegis. "You did right to bring her to me. One of those ribs could have punctured her lungs. She's a very lucky woman."

Aegis was sitting by my side, holding my good hand as if he'd never let go. "Can you give us a moment alone, Jordan?"

Jordan nodded, excusing himself.

Aegis turned to me. "I thought I was going to lose you." All of his pain and fear went into those words.

I squeezed his fingers. "I thought *I* was going to lose *you*. I don't know how Tom got free from the place I last saw him, but I never expected him to show up. I'd like to know what happened, but I doubt that I ever will. At least he's at rest now." Tears trickled down my cheeks. It felt like I'd cried more tonight than I had cried in my life. Than I had cried since Tom first was stolen away by the vamps.

"I'll see what I can find out," Aegis said. "Maddy, I don't know how to ask this but… How are you? I can't imagine what you're feeling."

"Numb. Just numb right now. I had put Tom behind me. I had let go and accepted that we'd never be together again. My heart had already said good-bye. When I saw him tonight, I realized that the Tom I had loved was truly gone forever. All I could think about was staying alive. And about saving you because he would have destroyed you. And he would have taken me into his world. It's going to take me some time to process through this."

Then it hit me—our wedding was in three weeks. "Oh crap. I wonder if I'll be able to handle our wedding. Not all the preparations are finished. I thought I'd be healed up by then, but now…" I started to cry again. "This is going to ruin everything."

"Steady, my love. Everything will be all right. I'll talk to Sandy and Max, and we'll figure out whatever we need to figure out. I don't care if we have to get married here in the hospital. I just want you to be my wife." He leaned down and gently pressed his lips against mine. "Maddy, you're my soul mate. I know we were together before. I've known you since the day I set eyes on you, though I couldn't figure out how or where we had met. I'm still not sure, but we've been together many times."

He began to sing, soft and low, and the song helped me drift off to sleep. Thanks to Aegis and the drugs, my slumber was easy, because I knew my love was watching out for me.

Not quite three weeks later, at five minutes before the stroke of midnight, Aegis and I and Sandy and Max sat on white benches in the middle of the snow, under clear skies and a silver crescent moon. All our friends were in attendance. Bubba sat on the bench to my left, and Luna sat on the other side next to Aegis. I wasn't able to stand yet without pain, but I could sit, and I was determined to get married on the day that we had planned for our wedding.

Delia was officiating, in a beautiful rose-gold gown with a black cloak around her shoulders. I had managed to fit into my dress even though it hurt going on, and Sandy was in hers, and we were stark and beautiful, shades of red against the backdrop of snow. Max's parents weren't there—Max had sent them packing after Sandy told him that she knew how they felt. They had left the same day they arrived.

I glanced at our maids of honor. To the left, next to Sandy and Max, Jenna stood, wearing a white chiffon gown and a rhinestone tiara. And to the right, next to Aegis and me, Fata Morgana was wearing a gown the color of the ocean depths, and her eyes sparkled like diamonds. Her hair was swept up in a chignon, the brilliant copper falling in coils to her back. She had come in off the ocean waves, more alien than before and yet—still, she was our beloved Fata, regal and every day growing into the goddess she was to become.

And once again, we were the *Witches Wild*. Perhaps for the last time, but for the moment, we were together, we three, united in a cause.

We had finished pledging our vows, we had promised to love as long as our love should last, and Delia was handing us the rings. As I slid Aegis's ring onto his finger, I looked into his face. All regrets over Tom were gone, and while I would always have my memories, everything felt settled and done. However long Aegis and I would have together, we would make it as joyous a union as possible.

I glanced over at Sandy, who looked as radiant as I felt. And when Aegis leaned in to kiss me, and Max leaned in to kiss Sandy, all felt right with the world.

We held the reception in the Bewitching Bedlam, so I could easily rest if I needed to.

I was seated in the rocking chair, and everybody was waiting on me hand and foot. Sandy sat next to me and we held hands. Fata Morgana had left early, after the ceremony. She kissed us both on our cheeks, and whispered that she would see us again on the spring tide. And then, she had vanished in a whirl of snowflakes, swept off by the wind to return to the ocean. It was hard losing her so soon. But like Tom, she no longer belonged to us. She had her own world.

"What are you thinking about?" Sandy asked.

"The people who have left us. The people we've left behind. Everything is so transitory. Even those things that seem like they should be anchors, eventually they can shatter and break. Or drift away on the tide to a new place and a new life. Life is about as stable as the earth herself, which can be pretty frightening you think about it." I gave her a smile and squeezed her fingers. My other wrist was strapped up, mostly healed by now, but it still ached.

"Long thoughts for our wedding day," Sandy said. "We lose people all the time, but that just means we need to embrace our loved ones all the more. Nobody knows how much time we are granted. Nobody knows how much time we have stretching out in front of us. I don't care how long-lived you are—whether you're a shifter or a vampire or a witch or a human. *Any day* could be the last day, so embrace life, and make it worthwhile."

I nodded, sipping champagne. "How's Jenna? I'm glad she was with us at our wedding."

"She's fine. I don't expect the rebellious phase to go away anytime soon, but we've come to an understanding for now. Oh, and Auntie Tautau wanted me to tell you that you did a good job on the Touchstone. Krampus made it home in time for Christmas, and the gnomes are back in the storybook, thank gods. They literally tore up my guest room with their rabble-rousing. I think I'd rather have *real* gnomes instead, even if they *are* more dangerous. And people are behaving themselves again."

"Oh good. You know, Franny found out who that ghost was. Apparently a man named Danny Irons disappeared a few weeks before the ghost showed up in our yard. He fell off one of the retaining walls and drowned. They just recovered his body, but Franny was able to help him remember who he was and how he had died. Now his family has closure, and he can move on. Franny's talking about setting up a service for ghosts who are stuck. I don't know how that's going to work, but we'll see."

"And *you*? How are you?" Sandy set her glass down. "Maddy, I know what a shock it had to have been when Tom showed up. By the way, I asked Auntie Tautau about that and she wouldn't tell me how he got free from wherever he was. She just said that everything that had happened was meant to be and to leave it alone."

I nodded. "I know. I asked her and she told me the same thing. As for me? I'm good. I'll be better when I finally heal up, but…I feel that I've finally fully let go of the past. And I'm married to the love of my life. The Bewitching Bedlam is going great guns, and I've decided it's time to really focus on my job as High Priestess. I intend to make the coven a *real* presence in the town. I'm not sure how yet, but I'll figure that out later."

A moment later, Sandy blushed. "I have something to tell you," she said.

I laughed. "Does it perhaps have something to do with the fact that you're drinking sparkling water instead of champagne?" I knew exactly what she was about to tell me. She wasn't my BFF for nothing.

"You know?" She shook her head. "I never thought I'd be saying these words, but yeah, I'm pregnant."

I finished off my drink and leaned back in the chair. "*Wow*. Look at us. Two old married women, and now you're pregnant. I'm so happy for you and Max." I grinned, catching her hand up to kiss her fingers. "I hope Aegis and I get to be the goddess-parents?"

"Of course!"

"Well, I'm just as happy it's you and not me, but I have some news as well. I'm going to be a grandma."

"What? A grandma?" Suddenly, she laughed as Bubba and Luna came bouncing up on my lap. "*Oh no.* But you had Luna spayed!"

"Apparently Bubba wanted to be a daddy, and Luna agreed, I guess. Somehow, she's intact, and yes, we're going to have a bunch of baby cjinns. Or maybe just kittens. Maybe both. I'm not sure how this works, but Luna is in good health and the vet said that she'll be giving birth in about a month. I'm not going to bother having her spayed again, because if Bubba wants more babies, Bubba's going to find a way. I just don't know how many cats we can take care of."

"Well, Mr. Peabody's lonely so I'll take a couple kittens—as long as they're not cjinns. I don't know if I could handle that. And Jenna would love it. You know how many people on this island would absolutely love to have one of Bubba's babies."

We settled back, then, into the party. Aegis and Max

sat nearby, protective and watchful, the most loving partners we could ever hope to have.

I looked around at the people who filled the walls of our home. Henry and our guests, all our friends, Franny and Bubba and Luna… Everyone who made up the fabric of our lives was here. And life was good. I decided to quit worrying about the future, and to leave the past where it belonged, and focus on the present, which was filled with laughter, and love.

Bubba looked up at me, and in his eyes, I could see that he fully agreed with me.

"Hey, Bub…bet you never expected to end up here, did you?"

Bubba let out a loud purr, and the party continued long into the night.

IF YOU ENJOYED THIS NOVELLA AND WANT TO READ THE REST of the series, then come meet the wild and magical residents of Bedlam in my Bewitching Bedlam Series. (Lighter-hearted but still steamy paranormal romance.) Fun-loving witch Maddy Gallowglass, her smoking-hot vampire lover Aegis, and their crazed cjinn Bubba (part djinn, all cat) rock it out in Bedlam, a magical town on a magical island. BEWITCHING BEDLAM, MAUDLIN'S MAYHEM, SIREN'S SONG, WITCHES WILD, CASTING CURSES, BEDLAM CALLING: A BEWITCHING BEDLAM ANTHOLOGY, BLOOD MUSIC, BLOOD VENGEANCE, TIGER TAILS, and Bubba's origin story—THE WISH FACTOR—are available.

Come run with The Wild Hunt. Darker urban fantasy/paranormal romance, the first ten books are out: THE SILVER STAG, OAK & THORNS, IRON BONES, A SHADOW OF CROWS, THE HALLOWED HUNT, THE SILVER MIST, WITCHING HOUR, WITCHING BONES, A SACRED MAGIC, and THE ETERNAL RETURN. Book 11—SUN BROKEN—and Book 12—WITCHING MOON—are available for preorder now. There will be more to come after that.

Return with me to Whisper Hollow, where spirits walk among the living, and the lake never gives up her dead. I've re-released AUTUMN THORNS and SHADOW SILENCE, as well as a new—the third—Whisper Hollow Book, THE PHANTOM QUEEN! Come join the darkly seductive world of Kerris Fellwater, a spirit shaman in the small lakeside community of Whisper Hollow.

I invite you to visit Fury's world. Bound to Hecate, Fury is a minor goddess, taking care of the Abominations who come off the World Tree. Books 1-5 are available now in the Fury Unbound Series : FURY RISING, FURY'S MAGIC, FURY AWAKENED, FURY CALLING, and FURY'S MANTLE.

For a dark, gritty, steamy series, try my world of The Indigo Court, where the long winter has come, and the Vampiric Fae are on the rise. The series is complete with NIGHT MYST, NIGHT VEIL, NIGHT SEEKER, NIGHT VISION, NIGHT'S END, and NIGHT SHIVERS.

If you like cozies with teeth, try my Chintz 'n China paranormal mysteries. The series is complete with: GHOST OF A CHANCE, LEGEND OF THE JADE DRAGON, MURDER UNDER A MYSTIC MOON, A

HARVEST OF BONES, ONE HEX OF A WEDDING, and a wrap-up novella: HOLIDAY SPIRITS.

The last Otherworld book—BLOOD BONDS—is available now.

For all of my work, both published and upcoming releases, see the Biography at the end of this book, or check out my website at Galenorn.com and be sure and sign up for my newsletter to receive news about all my new releases.

PLAYLIST

I often write to music, and here's the playlist I used for this book.

- **A.J. Roach:** Devil May Dance
- **Al Stewart:** Life in Dark Water
- **The Alan Parsons Project:** Breakdown; Can't Take it With You
- **Alice in Chains:** Man in the Box; Sunshine
- **The Asteroids Galaxy Tour:** X; Sunshine Coolin'; Heart Attack; Out of Frequency; Major
- **AWOLNATION:** Sail
- **Beck:** Broken Train; Devil's Haircut
- **The Black Angels:** Don't Play With Guns; Always Maybe; You're Mine; Phosphene Dream; Never/Ever; Indigo Meadow
- **Black Mountain:** Queens Will Play
- **Black Sabbath:** Lady Evil
- **Boom! Bap! Pow!:** Suit

- **Broken Bells:** The Ghost Inside
- **Cake:** Short Skirt/Long Jacket; The Distance
- **Clannad:** I See Red; Newgrange
- **The Clash:** Should I Stay or Should I Go
- **Cobra Verde:** Play with Fire
- **Crazy Town:** Butterfly
- **David & Steve Gordon:** Shaman's Drum Dance
- **Donovan:** Sunshine Superman; Season of the Witch
- **Eastern Sun And John Kelley:** Beautiful Being
- **Eels:** Souljacker Part 1
- **FC Kahuna:** Hayling
- **Foster the People:** Pumped Up Kicks
- **Gary Numan:** Down in the Park; Cars; Soul Protection; My World Storm; Dream Killer; Outland; Petals; Remember I Was Vapour; Praying to the Aliens; My Breathing
- **Godsmack:** Voodoo
- **Hedningarna:** Ukkonen; Juopolle Joutunut; Gorrlaus
- **The Hollies:** Long Cool Woman (In a Black Dress)
- **In Strict Confidence:** Snow White; Tiefer
- **Jessica Bates:** The Hanging Tree
- **Jethro Tull:** Overhang; Kelpie; Rare and Precious Chain; Something's on the Move; Old Ghosts; Dun Ringall
- **Julian Cope:** Charlotte Anne
- **The Kills:** Nail In My Coffin; You Don't Own The Road; Sour Cherry; DNA
- **Leonard Cohen:** The Future; You Want It Darker

PLAYLIST

- **Lorde:** Yellow Flicker Beat; Royals
- **Low with Tom and Andy:** Half Light
- **M.I.A.:** Bad Girls
- **Marilyn Manson:** Arma-Goddamn-Motherfuckin-Geddon; Personal Jesus; Tainted Love
- **Motherdrum:** Big Stomp
- **People In Planes:** Vampire
- **R.E.M.:** Drive
- **Rob Zombie:** Living Dead Girl; Never Gonna Stop
- **Saliva:** Ladies and Gentlemen
- **Seether:** Remedy
- **Shriekback:** Underwaterboys; Over the Wire; Big Fun; Dust and a Shadow; This Big Hush; Nemesis; Now These Days Are Gone; The King in the Tree; The Shining Path; Shovelheads; And the Rain; Wriggle and Drone; Church of the Louder Light
- **Spiral Dance:** Boys of Bedlam; Tarry Trousers
- **Steeleye Span:** Blackleg Miner; Rogues in a Nation; Cam Ye O'er Frae France
- **Tamaryn:** While You're Sleeping, I'm Dreaming; Violet's in a Pool
- **Tempest:** Raggle Taggle Gypsy; Mad Tom of Bedlam; Queen of Argyll; Nottamun Town; Black Jack Davy
- **Tom Petty:** Mary Jane's Last Dance
- **Tuatha Dea:** Kilts and Corsets; Morgan La Fey; Tuatha De Danaan; The Hum and the Shiver; Wisp of A Thing Part 1; Long Black Curl

- **Wendy Rule:** Let the Wind Blow; The Circle Song; Elemental Chant
- **Woodland:** Roots; First Melt; Witch's Cross; The Dragon; Morgana Moon; Mermaid
- **Yoko Kanno:** Lithium Flower
- **Zero 7:** In the Waiting Line

BIOGRAPHY

New York Times, Publishers Weekly, and USA Today bestselling author Yasmine Galenorn writes urban fantasy and paranormal romance, and is the author of more than sixty-five books, including the Wild Hunt Series, the Fury Unbound Series, the Bewitching Bedlam Series, the Indigo Court Series, and the Otherworld Series, among others. She's also written nonfiction metaphysical books. She is the 2011 Career Achievement Award Winner in Urban Fantasy, given by RT Magazine.

Yasmine has been in the Craft since 1980, is a shamanic witch and High Priestess. She describes her life as a blend of teacups and tattoos. She lives in Kirkland, WA, with her husband Samwise and their cats. Yasmine can be reached via her website at Galenorn.com.

Indie Releases Currently Available:

The Wild Hunt Series:
　　The Silver Stag

Oak & Thorns
Iron Bones
A Shadow of Crows
The Hallowed Hunt
The Silver Mist
Witching Hour
Witching Bones
A Sacred Magic
The Eternal Return
Sun Broken
Witching Moon

Whisper Hollow Series:
Autumn Thorns
Shadow Silence
The Phantom Queen

Bewitching Bedlam Series:
Bewitching Bedlam
Maudlin's Mayhem
Siren's Song
Witches Wild
Casting Curses
Demon's Delight
Bedlam Calling: A Bewitching Bedlam Anthology
The Wish Factor (a prequel short story)
Blood Music (a prequel novella)
Blood Vengeance (a Bewitching Bedlam novella)
Tiger Tails (a Bewitching Bedlam novella)

Fury Unbound Series:
Fury Rising

Fury's Magic
Fury Awakened
Fury Calling
Fury's Mantle

Indigo Court Series:
Night Myst
Night Veil
Night Seeker
Night Vision
Night's End
Night Shivers
Indigo Court Books, 1-3: Night Myst, Night Veil, Night Seeker (Boxed Set)
Indigo Court Books, 4-6: Night Vision, Night's End, Night Shivers (Boxed Set)

Otherworld Series:
Moon Shimmers
Harvest Song
Blood Bonds
Otherworld Tales: Volume 1
Otherworld Tales: Volume 2
For the rest of the Otherworld Series, see website at Galenorn.com.

Chintz 'n China Series:
Ghost of a Chance
Legend of the Jade Dragon
Murder Under a Mystic Moon
A Harvest of Bones
One Hex of a Wedding

Holiday Spirits
Chintz 'n China Books, 1 – 3: Ghost of a Chance, Legend of the Jade Dragon, Murder Under A Mystic Moon
Chintz 'n China Books, 4-6: A Harvest of Bones, One Hex of a Wedding, Holiday Spirits

Bath and Body Series (originally under the name India Ink):
Scent to Her Grave
A Blush With Death
Glossed and Found

Misc. Short Stories/Anthologies:
Once Upon a Kiss (short story: Princess Charming)
Once Upon a Curse (short story: Bones)

Magickal Nonfiction:
Embracing the Moon
Tarot Journeys

Printed in Great Britain
by Amazon